CW00521308

Praise for The Blood:

"This is a real page turner, a wonderful story with great action, plus a travelogue of Europe. Impressive!"

"Welcome, Mr. L.G. Rivera, to my list of 'must-read' authors."

"The book is fast-paced and takes you from horror to romance to adrenaline-pumping action with mastery. I was also surprised by the thorough research as well as the very relatable characters found on every page."

"I really enjoyed reading 'The Blood' and I would recommend it to anyone who likes a historically based great adventure story."

Also by L.G. Rivera

Sunk

The Blood

Z+

Short Stories:

Maggie Moo

The Life Coach

Coming Soon

Agobio

and

The exciting sequel to The Blood:

The Bones

DAMMED

L.G. Rivera

Published by Studio 223 Productions

Dammed. Copyright © 2010 by L.G. Rivera

All rights reserved under International and Pan-American Copyright
Conventions.
Published in the United States by Studio 223.

Cover Graphic Design by H.D. Bradford

Author Photo by T. Connelly

"Tiny Tiny Horse" Photo by L.G. Rivera

Library of Congress Cataloging-in-Publication Data
Rivera, L.G.
Dammed / L.G. Rivera.

ISBN 978-1490337555

Printed in the United States of America
First Edition Published in 2010 by Studio 223 Productions
Second Edition Published in 2013 by Studio 223 Productions

Studio 223
PRODUCTIONS

DAMMED

1
PLANS AND MACHINATIONS

I lay on the ground at the edge of the canal looking at the inky blackness below, staring at her face, pale and beautiful and slowly sinking. As the darkness swallowed her, my own face came into view, reflected in the murky water. For a moment, my face and her face became one. Her eyes were my eyes, and I could almost see myself, disheveled, spent, fixated on her. She sank slowly and disappeared as I lay watching. As the waters calmed, I stared at myself, at my reflection, and at Win standing over me. He smiled and turned, disappearing into the misty night. I cursed myself for having invited him, but it was inevitable. And the worst part was I knew he would do it again.

In the beginning, though, it all seemed a good idea. It started as all great and doomed ventures do, bellied up to a bar over entirely too many drinks. I was telling Win, my long time friend and sometimes partner in debaucheries, that I had just landed the sweetest honey of a travel-writing job ever. The boyfriend of a girlfriend of mine had seen an article about the trials and tribulations of Haiti that I'd written after traveling there on a wild National-Geographic-caliber adventure. The boyfriend, Frederick, happened to be working for a publisher of Christian books, of all things, and I told him after a wine-buzzed boozy evening dinner party of my idea for a series of Christian travel guides, which I perceived to be a void in the marketplace.

"I'll call them Road to . . . wherever," I told him and took another great gulp of my Pinot Gris. He loved the idea and ran with it.

I didn't hear anything about it for a long time and had almost forgotten about it until a call that afternoon, right before I met Win at the bar. Frederick asked me if I would like to write the first book and see how it was received. My heart leapt and I said "Hell yeah," only I didn't say hell, but golly yes or some other Leave-it-to-Beaverism that sounded fake coming out of my mouth.

"So, where?" I asked Frederick.

"Well, where do you know best? Where would you like to go?" he asked back, leaving the decision to me.

"Amsterdam," I said without hesitation or other thought. I probably knew other places better, though I had been to that gently sinking city a couple of times and the thought of spending a week there on someone else's dime was exciting beyond belief. So it was settled and contracts signed and sealed and I was going to Amsterdam. I told Win about it after work that day after a ton of Manhattans, surrounded by the rich wood paneling of the country club bar where he practically lived. I never saw him anywhere else, it seemed, unless we were traveling together.

Win, born Darwin J. Jones, though I called him Win, sat perched on a stool at a tall table in the bar, his long legs folded, and slapped me on my back.

"That's fuckin' awesome man – what a score, I'd love to go over there man, I mean I never been but I remember our last trip to Madrid and it was fuckin' great and I'm sure Amsterdam has to be ten times better man alive and fuck it!" he rifled out and slammed his big hands on the table, shaking empty glasses of melting ice and cherry stems, "I gotta go man I gotta go with you I gotta go that's all there is to it! I'm goin'!" Win's speech was always non-stop and he did not breathe ever while he spoke.

"That's great dude, that sounds like a plan," I said in a Maker's Mark-fueled boozy drawl. Everything and anything sounded like a great idea right then. It would be good to have him along, I foolishly thought at the time.

"Fuck yeah it is," he pounded my arm, "we're going to have fun you and I, fuckin' tear that place apart," he said, raising his voice. Some in the staid country club crowd – thankfully light at the moment – turned around to see what had defiled their silence. Win was excited and giddy as a schoolkid at the precipice of Christmas break, a natural exuberance that carried me along on its strong wave despite the harsh crass scratching edge that he had.

"Let's get outta here, man," I said. "I gotta get something to eat and I don't want to drop eighty dollars for a steak here."

"Fuck it man we gotta celebrate!" Win said excitedly, then gave a great big room filling *woot* and yelled loudly and simply, "Amsterdam!"

More heads turned now and I really wanted to leave. Country clubs in general – and this one in particular – always made me edgy, as if I didn't belong, and the members sensed my independent vibe and gave me nasty real or imagined looks. Win belonged here, for some unfathomable reason, and had convinced me to join. "It'll be good for business," he'd said. Part of me liked the opulence and money, but most of me felt uncomfortable. A necessary evil for business, I suppose, but an evil nonetheless.

I argued and we settled on a mid-upscale steak house not too far away and I had a good steak and we downed a couple of bottles of wine and we were drunk in earnest now. We closed down the place and Win drove like a rally car maniac entirely too fast and aggressively through quiet suburban Wednesday streets, getting right up on unsuspecting law abiding motorists, right up on them, up their tailpipe. We raced to a tiny bar near my house.

The bar was a real shithole full of honest hard-working stiffs and professionally unemployed disability vultures, neither category of which I fit. Neither one of us fit in the place really, me with my longish hippie hair and scruffy beard and college professor demeanor, and Win with his tall blonde curly-haired surfer good looks, which I secretly envied. I liked the place, though, as a last resort, some sort of final refuge of the damned before the hammer of judgment dropped down after long drunk nights and cruel searing light hangover mornings. Win tried to order a Pinot Grigio and the bartender, a sweet and pretty thing that had to have a hard edge to her to have landed here, didn't know what it was.

"They don't know what the fuck a Pinot Grigio is in a place like this," I whispered in Win's ear, "get a beer, ya snob." We sat and drank watery beer and tried to play pool in the tiny place.

Eventually, even that place closed and I walked home, leaving Win to terrorize anyone foolish enough to be out at this witching hour. I barely made it home before unloading my bladder and collapsing in bed.

It was a terrible puking night and I finally went to sleep at four a.m., waking up at six a.m. feeling absolutely terrible and wrecked. My grandmother was a circus acrobat and once fell from on high on her back onto a tent peg and that is exactly what my head felt like that morning. Tent pegged. But I had work to do and espresso angels helped me do it, and besides, I had plans and machinations for my upcoming Amsterdam trip. I still could not believe it and I called Frederick on the pretense of hammering out some details, though I really only wanted to make sure I was actually getting paid to go to Amsterdam. And I was.

I made all the arrangements and the next two weeks before the trip flowed like molasses in winter. I tried calling Win so I could confirm travel plans with him but he was distracted and on some other questionable venture at the time and he could not spare any of his mosquito attention span on me. It was all just as well, as he tended to bring nothing but trouble, a fact I constantly overlooked.

Win was mercifully quiet and absent from my life those two calm weeks before the trip until two days before when he called on me, showing up uninvited and unexpected right at my office.

"Dude, I've been making preparations and plans and what-not and this trip is coming up fast as hell and I'm completely unprepared," he said, interrupting my work, and continued even though I didn't look up. "Man I'm excited as hell and we gotta go to the bank *right now* today. Absolutely today. Right now."

"I gotta work dude," I told him, "look at all this shit." I pointed at the stack of unedited articles and manuscripts. "Deadlines."

"No go, man, you gotta come. If you don't go I don't go, and I need to go, so let's go," Win insisted. I was reluctant but Win persisted. "Come on man, we gotta go there now. We've got two days and I wanna be ready to hit the ground running. No excuses. And besides, bank's closed tomorrow so it's today or nothing and I don't want nothing so it's today," Win shot back at me and leaned over the table and slapped me on the arm. "Now. Let's go. Leave this shit for later."

"Fine," I succumbed, "but lets get a drink downstairs first." I would get nothing done now that Win was here, and if I was going to slack off on this, my last Friday before the trip, I would do it proper with a beer or three in my belly. Win was more tolerable liquored up anyway.

I locked the office and we went downstairs to a beer and pool joint on the ground floor of my building. It was practically deserted at two-thirty in the afternoon, with only a couple of professional drunks inhabiting the place and a surly dark-haired bartendress presiding over the whole sad affair. We got drinks.

"How can you drink that shit?" Win asked, pointing at my drink.

"I like it, man." I was drinking Guinness even though the girl didn't know how to pour it. She kept rushing the pour. I thought about educating her but she looked humorless and ill-tempered.

"If you say so," Win shook his head, then looked over the bartendress. "How about her?" Win tilted his whiskey glass at her.

"Her?" I looked at her and over at Win. "She'd cut you, man. You've got no chance with her," I whispered to Win. "Just look at her." The woman's face was frozen in a permanent scowl, as if the fates had dealt her an unkind hand, which they might have, for all I knew.

"She'd be a tough one," Win agreed, rubbing the blonde stubble on his chin.

"An uphill battle," I said, "Let it go. Be patient."

"Alright. Come on man. It's time. Let's get to that bank," Win said.

I was nicely buzzed from the Guinness, as I'd had nothing to eat. We drove fast, blazing through school zones and running yellows and pulling into the bank a half hour before closing. Win leapt out of the car, eager to get in there, pulling me along. We entered the lobby and put our name on the little sheet and soon we were ushered off to the vault on the side of the bank, to the safe deposit boxes.

Win took the key from his pocket and in a moment the box sat on the round table like a tiny metal coffin. He waited for the attendant to leave before opening it. He stared at the contents intently with big slate-gray eyes. I stood off to the side, a satellite.

"You get what you need yet, man?" I asked nervously. Banks made me uncomfortable and more so vaults like this. I could picture the massive steel doors swinging shut and being trapped with Win forever. We would have to fight for survival, eat each other to live.

"Not yet dude, give me a moment," I heard him say. I was starting to get lightheaded and the room closed in on me. Win took out a tiny 2" x 2" picture of a girl and stroked it with his long finger. The harsh bright halogens overhead reflected down, casting dark shadows over Win's normally handsome face and tinting it with a reddish glow from the reflection of something inside the box.

"Tricia Schiller," Win whispered under his breath and stared at the photo with glazed eyes. I stood off to the side, aching to leave. "Trish the German dish," he went on, softly, to himself. Win turned to me. "That was a good time in Berlin, wasn't it?" His voice was soft and calm and it sounded strange coming from him, as I was used to him yelling in my ear half the time. The box calmed him. It always did.

"Yeah that was a nice trip," I said absently. It had been a madcap boozy whirlwind through half of Germany years ago that I scarcely remembered, one of our first trips together. "You done yet?" I asked again. I was on edge now and the room really did seem to be closing in; hundreds of safe deposit boxes, like tiny niches of the dead, closing in around me in this mausoleum of money.

Win set the picture back in the box and rifled through other tiny pictures of other forgotten girls from other forgotten trips, smiling contentedly to himself. Finally, he brought out his passport and a wad of money from the box. Win closed it, sealing it with a metallic clang.

He looked at his passport again and scooped it and the wad of bills up and stuck them into his pocket. He pressed the button and the attendant came and the metal box went back into its empty slot, just another number now. Win flashed a smile at the attendant and he chatted with the cute and bookish woman. I had to get out though and left in a hurry and Win followed.

At last, we were out of the bank, standing in the baking August Florida sun.

"What now? Win asked.

"No use going back to work now," I said. We went off to an after work happy hour meat-market and prowled for office assistants and short-skirted paralegals into the late night hours.

I awoke the next morning wrecked but had work to work and responsibilities to be responsible for. The trip to Amsterdam was hurtling towards me now and I did what I had to do, finishing late and packing hastily the night before.

I didn't hear from Win that day and I wondered if he would show at the airport, and he did.

I drugged myself for the long flight, taking three Tylenol PMs and drinking a bunch of expensive drink at the airport bar before leaving. I settled in, comfortably wrapping myself in a cocoon of thin blankets. I hated these long flights. Thankfully, we sidestepped Hurricane Bill, which was pinwheeling through the Atlantic, and caught the winds just right and we were carried on God's own Mighty Breath, flying across the ocean in 6 short hours.

I woke up groggy and early, entirely too artificially early. The sun was coming up in crystal skies and we were so high I thought I could see the curvature of the Earth. We were soon over land and I hungered excitedly for Amsterdam. The descent took entirely too long, flying over patchwork quilt green farmland and small and large towns and now highways and tiny ant cars and now tiny model railroad trains and houses that rose and rose towards me as our plane descended. Landing gears whirred and popped out and the pilot gave a masterful performance landing, setting the big jet down so soft and light that the junction between air and ground could scarcely be felt. I wanted to clap and shake the pilots hand but everyone around me seemed not to notice.

After another fifteen minutes of interminable taxiing we arrived at the gate and Win awoke. He'd slept the whole flight, storing up his sleep like a winter bear that meant to stay awake for the summer. We waltzed through Dutch immigration, surprised at the laid-back attitude that comes in a country not trying to screw over every other country in the world. We breezed through customs and out into the terminal.

Schiphol is a wonder of an airport, radiating underground spokes that meet in a hub, the whole lot built on a drained sea and underground to boot. In no time I had my bearings and a wallet stuffed with Euro notes and a train ticket to the city proper. Win ran off at that exact moment and I waited for him in the huge central court, standing there watching a universe of people flow around me going in every imaginable direction. I felt great despite the long flight, happy to be somewhere different and I was anxious to get going. Finally Win came back.

"Where were you man? Let's go!" I said impatiently.

"Sorry man there was a cutie back there – man she was cute – back there at the flower shop that I just had to, – *had to!* – stop and admire and ask out. Man, oh man she didn't say much but she was fuckin' hot man, hot!" Win rifled out at me and punched me on the arm. "Let's go back man, I'm sure she has other hot blonde friends come on let's go," Win continued.

I glanced over his shoulder at the flower shop girl and she was indeed a stunner in a characteristic Dutch-flower-vendor-girl sort of way. She looked like she should be wearing a bonnet and blue and be milking cows.

"Nah, man," I said despite her good looks. "Let's get going. There'll be tons of chicks in Amsterdam. Be patient. Besides, she's not my type," I lied. The women who gravitated to me tended to be glass-wearing cute librarian types, or combat boot-wearing Nietzsche-reading pale-skinned cuties. However, I was not above a hot Dutch blonde. They were all my types, really. And there would be plenty of them in Amsterdam.

2
AMSTERDAM!

We hopped the train with our unwieldy luggage and silently set off. Soon, lights were flowing past and suddenly we broke forth out of the ground like a mighty earthworm and we were hurtling outside at speed on rails pointed to Amsterdam.

We pulled in to Centraal Station and instead of looking around for directions, I allowed myself to be carried in the great flow of people, rushing down gutters of humanity. We all spilled into a great underground river, which rose with a great will of its own out and out and out into a pale morning sun chilly dawn where old canal houses and great buildings caught us and we churned breathlessly at the mouth of this great city.

I stood a while like an obstinate pebble taking it all in while humanity swirled and flowed around me and then I was dislodged without thought or will of my own. We flowed along for a long time on the main spine of this river, down Damrak until it all broke at the Dam upon a great big stone obelisk with what looked like Christ floating crucified at the very center of it all, the weight of the great city upon His strong and tortured shoulders. People from every street converged on foot and bike and somehow no one ran into each other and it was amazing to me. I tried to stand still but, except for some tranquil eddies of gawking tourist groups, the crowd kept moving. I turned slightly and walked down another street to our hotel.

Tired, but wired awake, I only wanted to slough off my possessions and walk unencumbered. Soon, we had checked in despite it being so early. The pretty clerk put us in a single room, although we could pull the beds apart if we really insisted on it, she said, which we did. Right when I opened the door Win threw his things in and immediately darted right back out again on his long bicyclist legs. Before I could even register it – let alone call out to him – he was gone, out the door and the door after that. He could handle himself, surely. I just shook my head and went inside and stripped and showered and ran the hot water nice and strong and more life crept into my tired body as the film of travel washed down the drain. Soon, I was dressed in new clothes and was out the door myself with my still wet hair drying coldly on top of my head on a cool summer morning.

I picked a direction and started walking. I had no agenda, no one to meet or answer to, no problems that couldn't be put off till later, and I felt utterly fantastically alone. I walked down one of the main canals, the Herengracht, past rows and rows of gorgeous canal houses, big and opulent four-story affairs that lined the canals. I walked into ever smaller streets in a city only now waking, past quiet sleeping canal houses and closed fascinating shops of every conceivable specialization, including one that sold only ladybug patterned clothing and another of seals, as in signed sealed and delivered, not the aquatic mammal. I felt a light tingling like rain, though it was not raining, like a benevolent and kind electricity was guiding me along, floating. I was indescribably happy and felt so unworthily lucky to be here in this place on this perfect day. I stood at a corner, closed my eyes, and drank in that feeling. Every part of my body was alive and alight. Little pinpricks of that benevolent light hit my cheeks and face and kissed my solitude with their spirit.

I stood there a while, listening to the sounds, watching the clouds move and change and grow. I sat at a nearby bench under grey blue leaden skies which sheltered the old cobbled streets below. A myriad of people, each with their own designs and plans, flowed this way and that around me, like intricate clockwork circulating around this one corner. A duck hustled its way across the brown spoiled pea soup of the canal and found a temporary home and meal on a floating ancient algae covered log. Old anchors silently rusted and the weight of the city pressed down on the muck upon which it was built. A crazy houseboat sprouted ferns and trees and sad tropical plants pined for their jungle home and all the while a wooden outboard swayed alongside waiting for someone who would never come.

I took it all in, tired but refreshed by the shower and the change in latitude. Innumerable streets begged me to walk them, and though my feet hurt from long antiseptic airport walks, I did not care. It began to rain for real now, a light misty rain that I did not mind, and I sat there alone enjoying it. There was indescribable peace in the air and my real life seemed far from me as the East is from the West.

"Good fuck did you see that girl?!?" Win suddenly whispered in my ear behind me, shattering the peace of the scene and startling the hell out of me. He had materialized behind me, coming back from who knows what after he'd left the hotel.

"She was a hottie man, oh man alive! Did you see her riding that bike, man? That's so fuckin' hot," Win went on, louder now, punching my arm until I agreed with him.

The girl, eighteen at best, almost falling off the bike as her friend hopped on the back, was indeed a hottie. Despite myself I could not help but notice her nice firm young breasts as she bounced along her bike on the cobblestones. She regained her balance, turned and they rode off into memory.

"Win," I said, "she's young enough to be your daughter."

"Nah, man," he said a little too loudly, "she's good. Man all these girls here are hot. Fuck it man – I'm moving. Call home, tell them I ain't ever comin' back. There's bitches here to last forever."

I tried to tune him out. Bitches this and bitches that. Somewhere N.O.W. had a shooting range with Win's picture in the dead bulls-eye, pockmarked and shredded by lead. Win grew quiet again, like he often did when I tuned him out, which required some effort on my part. He could tell, and with no one around to listen to his misogynistic ramblings he withdrew into himself, thinking about God knows what in his hamster-wheel brain.

I sat in blessed silence again a moment and the city's heartbeat returned. Bicyclists clicking their chainy way past, the distant rumble of traffic, a seagull, and underneath it all, so quiet it could not be heard except in rare moments, the wind whistling through the leaves of still-green trees above.

"Let's go, man," I said. "Let's see what's out there." I desperately wanted to see the entire city, to walk everywhere all at once.

"Nah man, I'll catch up with you," Win said, smiling knowingly. "I've got things to plan and plans to attend to."

He split off in the direction of the bicycling girl, casting a look back at me and I caught a glint in his eye. He was up to something, I was sure, and I wanted no part of it in that peaceful morning. For once, though, the peace had won out and that was fine with me. He would be back. Of that, I was sure.

I walked down the broad canal street and the rain stopped. I walked on through smaller drying red-bricked streets going nowhere. At a pretty intersection I stopped and took in the scene. Sweet sad music poured out of one of the windows above me. In between beehive mopeds and cars rumbling by, in the temporary silence, beautiful music filled the air. I realized it was not a recording but some soulful girl and her guitar playing, pouring out herself so fully it filled her room and overflowed the window and the balcony and spilled onto the street and down on me. Cold pleasant shivers went through me as I took it all in, not wanting to spill a drop. I felt a little sad for the girl, for that was music born of sadness, and more than a little sad for all these poor folks walking obliviously by. Did they even hear her? Who was she and who was she playing for – herself? What was it that made her so sad? I wanted to yell out to her, have her come to the window, ask her out and build a life together but I didn't want to interrupt the music so I stood there and took it all in and let the world flow past for a little while.

She stopped after a spell and the street grew in its noise. Teen hooligans played in the park on the corner, pale Irish tourists walked by click-clicking with their suitcases, pink-clad teenage boys buzzed by on obnoxious insect mopeds. She had stopped and I wanted to call out to her and at least thank her for the sweet music, but what would she think of a foreign lunatic yelling out praises to her at her window? A mob of schoolchildren in uniform filed past and gave me strange looks, seeing this ragged and wet guy looking up at the balcony like a maniacal deranged Romeo, muted by fear and convention. I felt it best to move on before the sweet sad special moment changed or went away altogether. I instead stored it in my heart and vowed never to forget it or that sweet voice, but I knew I would and cruel time would swallow it whole.

I walked quiet backstreets devoid of tourists for a long time. I felt heady, high, and I had partaken in no controlled or uncontrolled substances, yet. I was high on the new surroundings and the lives of all the different people going every which way, making their lives in this old sinking city. A sense of peace and solitude permeated me and I sat on another bench at another canal and watched a duck and four beautiful swans and a strange squawking bird perched up on an outboard that looked like a miniature tugboat. I was happy. It had been a rough couple of weeks before the trip, full of booze and late nights and Win, and this respite here was much welcome. I felt like a bit of a fraud for taking on this doomed mission of writing a guidebook for Christians, of all things. But, in the still air around me, sitting on this peaceful canal, I thought I could actually do it.

I walked more and more and I began to think about lunch. It began to rain again, earnestly now, not the light kissing mist of before but an honest soaking rain that drove the umbrellaless indoors and under whatever free awning they could find.

The rain and the walking and the hunger were beginning to take their toll. The debaucheries of prior days were at my heels like a wolf stalking me. I did not know how long I could outrun them. Then, across the canal, I saw Win, walking, stoned and mellow and quiet. He saw me and his face lit up. He shouted at me, "Hey dude!"

"Meet me at the bridge," I shouted at him across the canal, pointing at the bridge at the end of the street. We were smack in the middle of the canal and for a moment I thought Win would jump in and swim across to me and, truth be told, the thought had occurred to me as well, though I dismissed it immediately as madness. Then Win did jump, but not in the canal but onto a decrepit ancient rowboat dating surely back to the turn of the century or earlier. He gave a great leap and landed big-footed square in the middle of the boat, helicoptering his arms wildly to regain his balance. I had visions of him going straight through the bottom of the boat like a Warner Brothers cartoon but the old planks held strong and true. Win began fiddling with the rope, meaning to somehow row across over to me without oars.

"You fool, get out of that thing," I yelled at him, mortified and looking around me.

"Quickest way across," he yelled back, patting his pockets for his knife to cut the rope, forgetting it had been confiscated at security. He worked on the complex sailor knots but in his happy stoned stupor his dexterity was lacking and also the rain conspired to make it difficult. Defeated, he climbed out of the boat, nearly falling in again, and began a sullen walk towards the bridge.

In no time we had merged and we walked together down the street, hands in pockets, faces scrunched and heads down, getting soaked by the rain. Several packed restaurants had no room for even one of us. Then, one dark and cozy restaurant welcomed us in with threadbare oriental rugs on the worn wooden tables and a great big empty ancient bar that ran the length of the place.

We ducked in and sat at the bar, taking two stools and waiting for service, watching the waitress furiously work on white bread sandwiches, grilling them on a small poor quality sandwich press. She was blonde and long and leggy and very Dutch, but she did not so much as look at us. We sat there longer, really thirsty now that beer was inches from us. A small dark Indonesian older lady walked in from a back room and took a few orders of other customers. Finally she came to us and I asked for a BLT and she launched into a long tirade and explanation about how she could not possibly serve up more sandwiches and was not taking any food orders – at this, a restaurant – as her cook was not here and on and on.

We took the hint and left. I assumed she did not want our kind in there, as Win did look pretty stoned and I myself was scruffy and my long hair was a crazy mat of wet fur on my head. Thinking about it, I should have been mad. Maybe I would have been, but the day had put me in a great mood and I welcomed something better than a sandwich made on substandard equipment by a poor harried waitress, no matter how cute. Something better surely waited for us out there.

We walked in the rain and it was pouring buckets now.

I said, "We need something soon, man, I'm about to pass out." I needed to sit, eat, regroup. The exhaustion had grabbed hold of my leg and was trying to take me down.

"In here," Win yelled back at me and we dragged our wet selves into a nice big restaurant with plenty of open tables. It was bright and cheery despite the dark wood and the brooding weather outside and the seats looked comfortable. We sat down on the padded chairs.

We ordered two beers and they were cold and delicious and pleasingly bitter.

"Look at this thing," Win complained, "all head, just a great fat head."

"That's how they serve it here," I responded.

"She hates me, that waitress," Win said, eyeing her maliciously from across the room.

"Calm down, paranoid," I told him. Win got mellow when he smoked, but sometimes waves of paranoia would wash over him. "It's all head here," I said, referring to the Dutch preference for a foamy top. "They like it that way. It's good, try it."

"These beers are tiny dammit," Win went on. "Is this some sick joke?"

"Stop bitching. Just drink more. Its all good," I said and took another sip of mine.

Finally, Win calmed down after downing a beer in one great swallow and getting another from the waitress who now eyed us suspiciously.

Mustard soup was the soup of the day and I asked the waitress what it was and she, unhelpfully, said it was a soup made with mustard. I was curious and decided to try it, as the rain had given me cravings for soup. I ordered the soup and a mozzarella and tomato and pesto sandwich and Win ordered another beer and no food, though he ate all the bread the waitress had brought out for my soup. He was always doing that – not ordering, then taking half or more of my meal, mostly without asking.

We ate with wild abandon. The soup was actually very good and the sandwich filling. I sat back, full and happy and drank another beer and took in the scene around me. A lonely man ate at the bar, reading a newspaper. Locals and tourists alike sat quietly and discussed in polite hushed tones. The sole exception was a loud American recounting all his tales of travels from the seven corners of the world and what country had bad nightlife and cocktails – Lebanon, apparently – and what was a cool place and what wasn't. I mean, who the hell goes to Lebanon for cocktails? I secretly wished curses on the guy and that he would return to South Beach where he probably was spawned. I was about to say something, but I let it all wash over me and enjoyed the rare silence from Win. I would have to keep him well drugged, slip pot brownies into his breakfast.

The sudden desire for sleep overpowered me, and I pushed it away. I had slept six hours in the past, what, 72, 84? No knowing now. It was all a hopeless mathematical blur of time zone additions and subtractions. It did not matter now, it was too late for that. Once past this state, the body will take care of itself.

"I want – no, need – to get me a nice fat black mama of a hooker," Win said from out of nowhere.

A couple of heads turned, though most politely did not look, but now listened to our table conversation intently.

"Later, man," I whispered. "There's plenty of time for all that." Then I added, "and why that? I would've thought you'd go for the Filipino chick or something tiny and Asian."

Win shook his head dismissively. "Ah, no no dude I've had all that. I've fucked a Filipino – a million Filipinos, man. I don't need that or need to pay for it." Win paused, then went on whispering in conspiratorial tones. "I've never fucked a huge black chick, and that's what I want, a great big fat black momma, man. I got a checklist right here," he pointed at the air, "of racial and body types and that's all I need to cross off, that's all."

I shook my head. "That's all you, dude. I'll just watch, uh, I mean wait. Wait I meant."

Win laughed and leaned across the table and hit my arm and then gave another great big laugh.

"See man, you want it," he laughed again, "you're so fuckin' curious man you at least wanna see it."

"I don't want to see you fuck a black girl, Win," I said deadpan.

Win laughed almost bending in half, caught his breath and wiped his eyes, he was laughing so hard.

"Lets get out of here," I said to him. Everyone in the place was looking at us now, at least it felt that way and probably was that way, with Win's great guffaws filling the place. "Let's go. Let's go find you your big fat black momma."

At this he gave a great big laugh and was crying and now people in the next room were looking over. I asked for the check and paid it tipping her a good American tip and we left. The rain had stopped and it was pleasingly cool outside.

"I'm going to the hotel," I told Win, overcome with tiredness.

"Fuck that, man, look at all these girls!" Win ogled a tall blonde a full head taller than he. "These are some of the finest bitches in the land and in the world here. Ain't no way I'm sleeping, no way – I'll sleep when I'm dead."

It was true. Win did not sleep, not much or not much that I saw anyway. For all I knew he could be coiled like a dormant viper when I was not around waiting to spring at my approaching footsteps. When I was around, he was always awake no matter what ungodly hour I got up and I could never outlast him into the night.

"You do what you need to do," I said. I needed to collapse and I'd rather do it into a nice bed than into the middle of a bike path in the middle of Amsterdam or, worse, face first into a canal. So I left him, and did just that, collapse into the bed that is.

The hotel's bed was the bed of kings, the kind that only good money buys, and this hotel was a class act all the way. I was frankly surprised that Frederick was letting me expense this out, but it was a relatively good deal so he let it slide. Plus, the drinks were free – even the booze – so maybe he was shrewdly hedging against an enormous minibar bill.

It was freezing in the room and the A/C was set on arctic blast, but I didn't care under the heavy down comforter envelope. My body spun into a warm cocoon where I hoped to metamorphose into the next incarnation of myself, rested and raring to roll, hopefully a little better person, and hopefully in the mood to get some of this work done and guidebook written. I slept the sleep of children and the sedated.

3
COFFEE AND T

When I awoke I was beautifully alone and Win was nowhere to be found. Probably already awake and out in the city somewhere, I imagined.

I left the hotel and it was cool and sunny out and people walked everywhere. There is a saying in the Netherlands that if you don't like the weather, wait ten minutes, and it was true, with each hour being like a whole new day. I passed by dozens of shops, all closed despite it being only 5:20 p.m. Stores in Amsterdam are all open from approximately one seventeen until about two o'five, at which point everyone either goes home or rides bicycles around town. And the hours are shorter in proportion to the good weather, so it is virtually impossible to determine ahead of time if any given shop will be open until you actually try the door. And who can blame them for leaving early? Perhaps they'd found enlightenment here and this riding around on heavy black bikes was the key. The bikes scared me. I wanted to ride one, but the seamless integration of all these bicycles without apparent signals of any kind led me to believe that maybe they were all part of some hive mind to which I was not privy, and my attempts to infiltrate it with my rented bike and my atrophied leg muscles were doomed. Still, I was determined to try.

I walked down quiet cross streets with delicious grandmother food smells cascading out the windows as innumerable moms or grandmoms cooked supper for their children. I was intensely homesick just then, if only for a moment. It was not a homesickness or yearning for my particular home, but something bigger, a timesickness, a longing to return to grandmother Yaya's chicken soup or the simplicity and beauty of the fried pork chop with tomato sauce she prepared. I wistfully remembered myself at six years old, legs dangling from tall dining room chairs, legs covered by that crocheted table cover safely sandwiched under glass, each delicate loop twisted together by old kind hands, the food a symphony of love and devotion and years of experience all concentrated into one sublime bite after another that I was too young or naïve to appreciate. Youth for all its follies is a treasure trove in which we store thoughts like this, to be opened later – a time capsule that makes you appreciate and miss those things you can never have again. Time is linear and relentless and the cruelest thing I know, an inexorable stomping of death camp boots marching us to open graves. Still, in the fleeting now, the street was quiet and beautiful and flowers spilled from tiny porches exuberant with life and all was well.

I was mistaken for a local about ten times, which I always secretly and pridefully love. One man spouted questions in French, asking for directions. I could not answer even though I spoke a smattering of the language. It did not matter, as I had no clue where I was much less where he was or was going to. A young couple shyly asked me if I knew where the Red Light District was and handed me a tourist map and I pointed them in some specific direction which was most likely wrong, sending them to untold adventures clear on the other side of town.

I made my way down to an art gallery which had some amazing photography of trees by a curious artist I had never heard of who I'd seen in a hotel "to do" magazine. After winding my way around I finally found it, but it was closed. Its opening hours read: Never. Blank a.m. to blank p.m. A sign read "Closed" in Dutch. I looked at what I could from the window and wondered at the nonexistent opening hours of this tiny gallery. Why have an exhibit and not exhibit it? Disappointed, and with absolutely nothing for my guidebook so far, I went to a corner bar and sat outside in waning late sunlight on a now absolutely perfect long summer day and watched life go by and drank a tiny Heineken.

I still needed to go to some sights, take some notes and pictures, and generally do what I had been sent here for and paid to do. I did not want to, though. Irresistible procrastination took over; I would sit outside on a fine day like this forever if I could. Then, at that peaceful moment, I heard a loud *woot* in the distance and turned and saw Win coming at me. I'd stopped moving and he'd caught up. I knew my peace was at an end. He bounded towards me, hurdled a leg over the back of the chair and sat at my table, drinking the rest of my beer. We ordered two more.

"What've you been up to?" I asked.

"Man, there are some tall and nice looking bitches here, man alive," he said and various Dutchmen at the next table turned and looked to see who was spouting such derogatory statements of their womenfolk.

"I mean look," Win slapped my arm, "look at those two hotties on a bike." He pointed at two girls, one riding sidesaddle perfectly balanced on the back of a bike. "Man I love that, that's the shit." He pronounced "shit" *shi-ite*, like the branch of Islam instead of its more common scatological pronunciation. I sighed and began to say something but he cut me off.

"Man, we need to get outta here we need to go to the fuckin' Red Light man, get you some weed, get you loosed up and fucked up man," he said.

"I'm loose enough," I said. "You're the one that needs to relax. Look at you, geez, you're a nervous mess." I pointed at his leg which jackhammered restlessly and constantly. It was a nervous condition he had and it occasionally drove me batshit, especially in quiet environments that Win was ill suited to anyway.

"Let's go man, it's drugs time," he insisted and punched me on the arm again.

I said, "Fine," and got up and paid for the beers. We walked down about three streets and found a respectable and clean coffeeshop with crazy nautical scenes and real coral on the walls – dark and blue and inviting. Win pulled me in and then jumped right back out, an action that surely would have been comical to anyone watching.

He said, "Wait, we need a pipe," and darted off and over to a curious smartshop on the corner where they sold a hundred thousand different pipes in every size and permutation known to man. The ingenuity of stoners to find ways to smoke cannot be underestimated. Soon, Win came back out carrying a small brown paper bag and he loped back to me on his long legs. We went back inside the nautical coffeeshop, for good this time. Win bellied up to the bar and ordered a selection of weed from the menu along with some orange juice from a pretty Arabic bartender with gorgeous dark almond eyes. We sat on a stool at the bar and smoked.

It was a cool scene in there, with chilled-out reggae playing on a good stereo and the air was not too smoky and it was not too crowded. We sat and smoked, and it was good. We were quiet, mellow and dug the Bob Marley. The weed calmed Win down.

Breaking the mellow vibe, a fat Chinese girl all big and goofy smiles came in with orb-like headphones around her neck blasting out *The Boys of Summer* so loud that they actually drowned out the chill reggae on the stereo and soon Don Henley was firmly in charge and Marley sat in the back. The cute waitress, smiling politely but all business, gave the fat Chinese chick a nasty look but she was all smiles and noticed nothing. China girl finally turned the headphones down on her own. I shuddered to think of those evil things against her ears. Drowning out the entire world, sure. But with *Boys of Summer*? To each her own.

She scored what she wanted and left. Next a timid man-child came up and ordered, in tentative steps, a succession of menu items until he ended minutes later with a pure weed joint in addition to almost everything else on the menu. The guy, a short skinny dude with very combed and neat lawyer hair, went back to his table by the window, juggling everything and setting it down slowly. At his table was sitting a leggy brunette, stunning and gorgeous, wearing a tight but tasteful elegant black dress, with beautiful and piercing blue eyes.

Win and I sat there and smoked what was very good high quality shit, really stony stuff that made you what to sit forever and stare off into space and enjoy nothingness. I stared out the window past the leggy brunette for what seemed like hours, and every once in a while I would catch the brunette looking back at me. She probably thought I was staring at her, which I wasn't, but after she looked over a few times

I *did* start to stare at her. She was a looker. Her smooth toned legs were well on display with the little black number she was wearing and she wore a large "O" necklace that hung like a target between her large breasts. Stoned as I was, it took great effort to peel my eyes away.

I looked over at Win and he was staring intently and maliciously at the little man sitting with her.

"What the fuck is that guy doing with her, man?" Win asked slowly.

"Bought and paid for is my guess," I said. "No one comes to a coffeeshop in a cocktail dress."

"She's looking hot, man," Win said. "How much money you got?"

"Not enough for that," I said and now I began to feel strange, swimmy, like something was splashing around inside me. It had been a while since I'd smoked and it was going to my head.

"I should get rid of that little fucker," Win said, going back to throwing eye daggers at the guy. "Have me a nice good night out on the town with that hottie, man."

"You leave that fucker alone," I told Win. "The guy's got enough trouble with a woman like that." A woman like that would make you bleed one way or another.

I sat there and alternated between looking at the couple and trying to look anywhere *but* the couple, looking instead at the wild coral reef interior. After a while, the little guy got up and walked past us, studiously avoiding our gaze, and went to the bathroom. The leggy brunette sat there, bored, looking out the window, up at the ceiling, and back.

Win leapt up from the barstool suddenly and walked to the bathroom, following the little guy. It was so sudden and I was so stoned that I didn't realize it until he was almost through the door. I fumbled with my pipe and looked over at the gorgeous brunette who was now sitting alone and gave her a weak smile.

In no time at all Win came out of the bathroom and walked right past me and straight to the brunette, covering the distance in a few steps. He sat down at the little man's chair, flashed his big Win smile and shook hands with her. I could barely hear them above Bob Marley, but soon the brunette was all smiles and Win was talking animatedly. She gave a great all-teeth toothpaste-ad laugh and I sat there and wondered how the hell Win could do that. If I'd tried the same thing, the woman would have called for security, I was sure. They sat talking and laughing for what seemed like a long time, which was hard to know in my pleasantly stoned state. The little guy was gone in that bathroom forever. I pictured bullies locking him in and giving him swirlies in the toilet.

Win and the brunette got up. She was very tall and looked even more stunning standing. She walked over to me prowling like a model on a catwalk, Win leading her over to the bar.

"This is Jenna," Win introduced us. "Jenna and I are going to go have a drink in this great bar that she knows and we're gonna have martinis and cocktails and then I'm going to teach Jenna here how to mambo and then we'll see what we see," Win said and turned and winked at Jenna.

I stared at them dumbly, distant, and said nothing.

"You wait right here buddy," Win said but he was far away already and I didn't mind as I was pretty well grounded where I was, feeling like a potted plant.

They turned and walked out the door, Win's long arm coiled around her small waist. The little bell on the door tinkled once and just like that they were gone. I twisted in my stool and asked the waitress for another orange juice and she gave me a sideways smile and raised eyebrow, and I shrugged. I was so stoned I felt like I wasn't there at all.

I smoked some more and my vision grew fuzzy and indistinct. Through clouded eyes I thought I imagined the little man coming out of the bathroom and looking at his empty table and then around the bar and then sitting back down. He sat there a while, staring at the bathroom door, probably thinking she was in there. I sat and drank my orange juice, listening to reggae, and, truth be told, feeling more than a little sorry for the guy. Someone should tell him, but what would I say?

My friend ran off with your girl there, don't worry, he'll be done with her soon? Not likely. Instead I ignored him and dug the music and smoked every once in a while, filling the little pipe with a tiny amount of the strong pot, then wastefully emptying it out after one puff.

It began to grow dark and the little guy finally left with an exasperated and confused look on his face. I must have switched chairs and tables a dozen times as I haunted the place waiting for Win to return from whatever raunch he was having with that brunette. A hundred different people came and went, some staying for a bit, most only picking up a gram or two and leaving. I kept ordering drinks. I had tipped the pretty waitress good solid American tips, so she didn't mind my loitering. My stomach was raw from orange juice and I switched to tea. At last, Win bounded in through the door, all smiles, sending the little bell dinging crazily as he swung the door open.

"Ooo wee," he said, sitting down by me. I had migrated to the window table now and was sitting in the same seat that the brunette had occupied.

"Man, that was one fine specimen of woman – she was a delish dish, I tell you," Win said and punched me in the arm.

"Good man, glad you had fun," I told him. "Where the hell did you all go? I've been waiting here forever." I complained but, like I said, I didn't really mind.

"Oh man, that bitch was a class act all the way, we went to this very fine establishment at a ritzy hotel a little ways away and had drinks there, good fuck they were expensive, but good, and I naturally charmed the pants off her," Win said and gave a big toothy smile, "or the skirt, I should say. We had a little fun there at the bar and over the railing of a bridge and she had a room there at that hotel and she was a minx, man," he punched me on the arm again, "a fuckin' minx she was."

"How the fuck you do that?" I asked him.

"Trade secret, buddy," he laughed.

"Let's get the fuck out of here," I said, "but let me go to the bathroom first."

I got up and walked through honey to get to the bathroom. The waitress shot me a smile.

"Back?" she asked.

"Never left," I told her and tried to smile but I already was smiling and my face hurt.

My body was numb it had been stoned so long, and my head was still about two steps behind me, like I had left it sitting on the table with Win. I went into the tiny bathroom, which was smaller than a closet, with a sink in the first tiny room and a door and then a second room, which was locked. I thought about pissing in the sink, but was afraid someone would walk in.

I really had to go with a vengeance and I tried the door again, jiggling it wildly back and forth, and no one called out or protested, and this time the door slid open with some effort. There was someone in there though and I immediately started sliding it shut again, then caught myself and did a double take. It was the little man-child that had been with the leggy brunette. *What the fuck*? I thought to myself. I could have sworn I'd seen the guy leave the coffeeshop. I looked, and his eyes were closed and he looked unconscious or at least pretty out of it. Or maybe even dead. I stood there for a second, puzzled and confused. My head swam and there was an insect buzzing in my skull, there for a moment then gone. I didn't know what to think. Strange things happen when you're stoned, a friend of mine used to say. Maybe I hadn't seen the guy come back. Who knows?

Still a bit shaken, I slid the door closed again. I splashed water on my face and looked at the polished metal over the tiny sink, my face all scratchy and distorted like a funhouse mirror. I needed to get out of there, get some air, get far away. My head swam again and I leaned on the sink for a second.

I caught hold of myself and walked out. Win was flirting with the waitress.

"Let's go, man, like right now," I told him and he peeled himself away from the waitress and we got out of there, the little bell ringing crazily as we swung the door open. I was free at last from the coffeeshop and out into nice cool night air again. It was beautifully refreshing to be outside again and we walked along for some time as my body came back down to earth.

I told Win about the little guy in the bathroom.

"Well thanks for keeping him busy for me, buddy," Win said and smiled a huge Cheshire Cat grin.

"I didn't do anything," I told him, "just found him in there. It was strange as fuck, man, I could've sworn I saw him leave the place."

"Sure, sure," Win said and shot me another devilish smile. "Like I said, thanks for taking care of him for me."

Thinking better than to dwell on it, I calmly let the matter drop. I shrugged and we walked on in silence, down Leidsestraat with its expensive designer shops, all closed. There were a ton of people out walking up and down the street, and every once in a while a tram would clang its way past. The street looked like Main Street USA in Disney World. It was surreal.

"We need pancakes, bitch, that's what we need," Win suddenly said, apropos of nothing. I was hungry, I realized, which made me hungrier.

"Yeah food sounds good, but what poor lunatic would have pancakes at this hour?" I asked.

"It's a reasonable hour," Win said, and it occurred to me I had no idea of the time, only that it was late. I looked up at a church's clock tower in the distance. Almost midnight. Good shit. Had I been in there that long swimming among the corals? It felt like five minutes and five days all at the same time.

"This isn't America," I said, "you just can't walk into a Denny's drunk and stoned at any hour of the day or night. All things but falafel stands close here at some point."

Win looked sullen with my bring-down, and we walked on, finally spotting a tiny still open restaurant with some patrons still in it. I refused to eat at any empty restaurants, even if still open. It was a cardinal rule of mine.

We sat and ate, basking in the total indifference of the waitress who was waiting for us, and everyone else, to leave. The tiny tips offered here make for complete apathy of waitstaff, and it was a self-fulfilling cycle. Only the promise of a paycheck could flog this girl on, and it wasn't coming from us so she did not care. I quickly ate, or drank rather, a bowl of watery chicken soup and Win ate nothing, with not even any bread present or even offered for him to pilfer. He sat there quietly while I ate.

We ended the night back at the hotel while a strange fat Arab and his young effeminate lithe companion checked in while we drank free booze in the lobby. We overheard the front desk checking them into room 11, right next to us.

Win whispered in my ear, letting me in about this fat Arab and weaving vast conspiracies that included him spying in on us from two way mirrors and keeping tabs and detailed records on our drug use and what we took from the minibar. "He'll surely use his newfound knowledge to sell you or a family member or loved one into white slavery, you know," Win whispered. "You gotta watch these satanic Arab fucks, you know – watch them with eagle eyes," he continued.

When we got back to the room Win covered all the mirrors, hanging clothes and towels everywhere and inspected the room for peepholes before disappearing into the bathroom with two beers and a gram of hash. He did not come out and I fell into a deep exhausted sleep.

Wolves howled in a Grimm Brothers forest and I slept soundlessly against a brooding tall tree. I rolled over and the little man from the coffeeshop was there, lying dead next to me. I hugged him as I would a pillow and felt the death chill of the body and was paralyzed, as if the death was leaching from him into me. Wolves howled in great baying infernal melodies, closing. A snarl right against my ear woke me up with a start and I rose up in bed but could still smell death and decay from dripping meat jaws and another snarl from behind me made me twirl around and a smiling fat Arab holding a severed snarling wolf head was behind me no matter where I turned and then I woke up for real with a great convulsion and I was in bed sweating in the dark room. I looked around but all was dark and quiet and only the sliver of a light shone underneath the bathroom door. Sweating against the pillow, I fluffed it up and breathed in and tried to forget the horrible night vision and go back to sleep. I lay there awake, hearing only the smallest splashing of water from the bathroom in the darkness. I finally drifted off again, but it was not for a long time, and it was a fitful sleep.

4
AROUND THE CHURCH

I got up the next morning only to find Win gone and a note reading, simply, "Estherea" scrawled on hotel stationary in Win's huge handwriting jammed into the frame of the mirror in the bathroom. I went downstairs for breakfast, pondering this cryptic message, but it was too late and it was closed and the large Filipino or Indonesian attendant would not let me grab anything at all to eat, even jealously guarding a basket of uneaten slices of bread sitting right there. Dejected, I went up to the lobby and googled Estherea and found it was another hotel not too far from this one. I went back to the room, saw that Win had cleared out the minibar, and, on instinct – and because the Indonesian had pissed me off by not letting me have any bread – packed and headed to Esthera. I found it, walked in and Win was sitting regally on a rich overstuffed sofa in the lobby of this grand fine establishment, legs crossed and arms spread out, taking up the entire sofa. He dressed in 1970's hip, new old clothes from some vintage store somewhere.

"Hey man," I asked, "what gives? Why did you take off? Why this place?"

"There was, how shall I put it?" Win ran his hand across his face, continuing, "An unfortunate incident at breakfast which was entirely not my fault with some bitch cunt lunchlady-large motherfucker of a waitress down there and she and I didn't get along too well and, well, I thought it was best to leave *muy pronto*." He looked at me with an air of complete confidence.

I took his word for it and settled into our place here, which was a far superior establishment anyway, much too nice for the likes of us and the monkey shit insanity we would no doubt wreak on the place. I worried when on the ride up the elevator to our room I saw the sign banning the use of cannabis products at the risk of a high monetary penalty. This was no mere paper sign either, but an engraved in brass number that told you they meant business. Win would violate this no doubt if he hadn't already, though it remained to be seen if we would get caught.

"I gotta do some work," I told Win while settling into our new digs. "I have got to get some sights in for this guidebook." The very reason I was here was starting to evaporate.

"Blah, blah, blah," Win dismissed me. "I'll catch up with you, man, I'm not into all that sightseeing crap and all," he said, then sat down in a chair and fell asleep in an instant, one of the few times I have ever seen him sleep, as if someone had turned off a switch. I quietly closed the door and snuck out.

I went out into a frightfully gorgeous summer Amsterdam sunny day with trees rustling and waving their leaves as if celebrating creation itself. I had coffee and apple pie for late breakfast at a tiny bakery and soon I had fuel for the day. I let the path of the ground guide me, going nowhere in particular and ended up going through a nondescript door to the cultured beautiful and quiet Beninghof, an old nun's convent turned into exclusive residences for the wealthy, an oasis of peace and quiet to those who could afford it. I wandered into a small church there and sat, letting the silence fill me. This was Guidebook for Christians fodder stuff for sure. *Observe if you would the detail of the altarpiece and the engravings on the chalice dating back to the 17th Century,* and so on. I took notes.

Small packs of tourists wandered in and out, snapping pictures, documenting their presence for posterity, viewing this grand church through two-inch viewfinders. Intricate smooth marble carvings encrusted with gilded gold angel wings flanked fresh flowers on a last supper altar. Christ hung above it, tiny and dead on a wooden cross, and He also stood above it all, huge and triumphant and encased in dead marble. A couple sat near me, the only others sitting down. They embraced quietly and tenderly, the tiny woman nestled into her man, hands clasped with hers stroking his tenderly, motherly, as if soothing some great hurt here in the quiet and solitude of this small silent and holy place in the middle of trams and bicycles and madness outside. It was a touching scene and I felt like a voyeur watching – I supposed I was – but it made me feel at peace too, knowing that there was some place of solace out there, some place to come back to and recharge. Some place to be alone. A giant tidal wave of tourists washed in at that moment and cell phones rang and defiled the peace and sanctity. It was time to leave.

I went out and got caught in the river of consumers eroding their way through the canyons of old city streets. I tried to fight the river but was caught in its pull and it took me, spilling me out at Dam again and inevitably, where logjams of humanity converged and flowed out to innumerable tributary streets and Christ still hung patiently suffering in the center. A tiny alley sucked me in; a grubby guitar-wielding Rastafarian gypsy salmoned his way upstream towards me. The Rastafarian gypsy smiled at me and said, "Hey mon," and walked on. The wind whistled through the dark alley and again I was the only one there. Blessed solitude. Leaves of garbage picked up by the breathy wind danced in joy before settling to be trampled underfoot. The alley spit me out onto the brackish tea-dark canals of busy Ouderzijds Voorburgwal, the Red Light District. I thought I saw Win out of the corner of my eye, his striking blonde head large and bobbing above the crowd but he – if it was him – had disappeared by the time I wound my way up the street and arrived at the Old Church.

The Old Church was perfect for my travel guide. I stood outside the edifice and took a picture. I walked in, but not before paying 5 Euros. "You need money to be a Christian in this town," I wrote in my notes. Inside, past massive wood-carved doors, I heard Bach on an organ and smiled. Walking inside, the church was huge and cool and monster octopus gold chandeliers hung from impossible black poles reaching to the vaulted wood ceiling six miles above me. The organ swelled in high registers and the music soared and climbed like an eagle in thermals towards some lofty cloud high above, then, like low alien trumpets of the apocalypse, the big pipes opened up and punched me in the heart, making my insides hurt and feel good all at the same time. For a moment, the Bach was grand and I was riding that eagle and my face was cool from misty clouds and my eyes were shut but lit up with pure golden sunlight streaming and warming me against the cold. A huge chord vibrated the entire place for a time and then ended, but not all at once. Its echo rang in the sudden silence for all eternity – if you could be quiet enough, you could listen to it forever. I thought about the centuries gone by in this place and the floating echoes of the past as the resolving C rang and rang and rang until low whispered voices and slamming doors and a worker pounding some stone somewhere finally drowned it out, and it disappeared like a jet through the air over the horizon and it was out of sight forever.

The organ, silent now, sat and loomed over the entire place like a giant many-fanged benevolent monster ready to bellow forth life and light from its myriad mouths. Outside, the church bell rang one o'clock. Win was out there someplace, not able to stand the stillness and peace in here. I walked through the church on the stones of the dead buried everywhere. The entire beautiful place was a huge graveyard, and the dead laid, waiting, their dust dancing below to the huge vibrations of the monster organ, then growing still, waiting again for any movement until eternity came. Without the music, the place was empty and sad, hollow and lonely. A tiny Christ hung from a wooden cross over the altar, out of proportion to the grandness around him. He looked on, forlorn, with small wood eyes surveying the emptiness around Him.

I walked out of the sad large church onto depraved cobblestone vice streets peddling hookers and drugs. I saw Win sitting outside at the Old Church Coffeeshop (most definitely not associated with the Old Church proper) and chatting with two beautiful – probably American – blondes. He saw me and motioned me over wildly and I stood there at the entrance to the patio, smelling the rich burnt leaf marijuana smell wafting over every time some joker opened the door.

"Dude, come on over here," Win said leaping out of his chair bounding over and dragging me to their table.

"Hey man, meet Monica and Jessica, they're from Georgia, Atlanta specifically, and this is their first –first! – coffeeshop and Amsterdam experience in general! Can you believe it, man? I told them I can show them around get them into the best clubs and restaurants, I know a ton of people and contacts here, its gonna be the shit man, give me the card from the hotel the little card you picked up," he waved his hands excitedly, "that hotel hell yeah it's the shit the best hotel ever nothing but penthouses and corvettes for these southern belles here, give me that card man." Win took a breath.

I fished around my pocket and handed him a card. I always carried one around after utterly erasing my memory in this stony city on a previous trip and actually not knowing for hours not only where my hotel was but the room or even the name of the place. Win gave it to one of the girls, either Monica or Jessica, I wasn't sure which one was which and hadn't paid attention.

Win turned to the girls. "Call me tonight, tonight at, what time is it now?" he asked the air.

"'Bout two," I said glancing at the massive clock tower on the church in front of us.

"Eight, call me at eight I'll be there and we're gonna go all bling bling on Amsterdam, best clubs restaurants no one can get into, VIP shit okay, so call, call me, okay call at eight."

One of the girls giggled, taking the card and putting it her fanny pack. Real tourists, these. I worried for them. In truth, we should stay with them to make sure they didn't get mugged or sold into white slavery or worse. Though one of them, Jessica I think, did look beefy with a field hockey player build, so they could probably handle themselves. Win stepped over the railing of the coffeeshop terrace with his long legs.

"Come on," he said, waving his arm frantically, "come here, come here!"

I had only just sat down and now got up. I waved goodbye to the two girls who were talking to each other and didn't notice me and went over to Win. He pulled me along the backside of the Old Church where despondent black women of every shade and size sat in lonely red windows. One of them, a great big fat and attractive – in a matronly way – black lady tapped on the window and beckoned us over, suddenly flashing a wide island smile.

"This is it man, this is what I was telling you I wanted to do here, right here and now right in front of us here it is!" Win rattled off excitedly. He was as excited as a twelve year old schoolgirl getting a pony for Christmas.

"What, the black chick, for real?" I asked, glancing in her direction as she stood there smiling and winking.

"Yeah man!" Win punched me in the arm in the same exact place every time and it was a bit sore. "I gotta do it. It's here and it's in front of me and I gotta do it." He paused. "I'll get you one of her friends."

Before I could object or protest he was at her door, which was cracked open in a conspiratorial sliver. She smiled and then laughed then put up one finger in a "wait here" gesture and opened a door behind her, disappeared for a time and then came back. Win pulled out a wad of bills, he never carried a wallet just a wad of bills held in check with an office black clip binder, handed her an unspecified amount of Euros and beckoned me over. He walked in the door. Win's sheer exuberance and force of will took hold of me, and reluctantly and against my better judgment – or any kind of judgment really – I walked through the door.

I walked in slowly, as if in a dream, squeezing through the tiny narrow door and feeling the eyes of a thousand around me. I followed Win down a tiny hallway and he in turn followed the large black woman, who wore nothing more than a loose fitting nightgown. We came to a door on the right; a hand-scrawled paper on it read "Destiny." The black woman, Destiny I assumed, opened it and walked in, then Win walked in. I stood at the door for one stupid moment, then Win turned to me in the darkness of the dimly lit hall and said simply, "Me first," then closed the door in my face.

I felt like an idiot standing in the hallway and more so for having let Win talk me into this. I sat on the grimy ground and put my head on my knees, hoping no one else would walk by.

There was laughing and then loud moans and thumps coming from the room. Soon Win was yelling and I could hear his muffled voice through the thin walls calling out and yelling lewd things at the prostitute. I secretly hoped she didn't understand enough English to understand the filth pouring out of Win's mouth, horrible words of degradation and insult.

I closed my eyes but my happy place was nowhere to be found. I was almost rocking back and forth when a loud thump shook the wall behind me. I shot up, almost jumping outside myself. I had to get out. I rose too fast, though, and my head swam and I leaned against the peeling wallpaper of the tiny hallway. In my confusion I got turned around and went the wrong way and opened a door I thought led outside and instead walked into one of the window rooms with a shocked as hell large black woman standing there looking at me. I apologized and turned around but she composed herself and came over and grabbed my hand, leading me into the room. As I looked at her, it was my turn to be shocked. She was a dead ringer for Win's Destiny, an exact twin. She closed the curtains and the room was bathed in velvet red light. She smiled at me and patted the bed built right into the wall, motioning to me to sit down. I just stood in front of her, detached.

Everything was happening slow and dreamlike. I looked on this black woman with a large round kind sad face, who asked me what I wanted. For a long time I did not say anything and I stood in front of her. My head swam again and I wavered. Then, on impulse and out of necessity, I had her sit on the bed and I knelt in front of her and hugged her warm legs and just knelt there. I put my head in her lap and told her to relax, I didn't want to do anything, I just wanted to sit there and relax and be alone and have her relax. I could sense her looking at me questioningly then she softened and I could feel her relax in her legs, which became soft pillows for my head. Soon, after a couple of minutes, she started stroking my hair softly and tenderly, maternally.

I could hear her sniffling and, even though my head was facing away from her and I was looking at the red curtains haloed in light, I knew that she was crying and now I heard her cry a little more, then a lot, then I felt like I was crying, but only dry tears came out. I thought about this sad little room and this foreign black lady from who knows what exotic jungle country sitting here day after day; I thought about long lonely walks home to wherever she lived or – even worse – maybe she never left this building. I thought of all this and soon I was crying in earnest like I hadn't done since my dear high school sweetheart died in some mysterious accident. I cried and I wept and my tears dripped down her legs and bathed her feet and I wiped them off tenderly. She continued stroking my hair softly and we sat there in silence together, united by some great cosmic sadness. We stayed like that for who knows how long and my knees ached and I moved. We had stopped crying, the two of us, and I wiped the rest of my tears from her legs and feet and she smiled and I sat there and smiled back.

I told her suddenly about the Old Church next door and the graves lining the floor and the great mighty monster organ bellowing Bach and the tiny dead Christ that hung sadly watching it all. She told me in her broken island English patois that she sometimes heard that organ and could even feel it vibrating her window in a low melodious rumble, a great celestial mighty resolving C that shook the world and radiated out to the deepest dark. I could picture her sitting alone here in this glassed-in cage gently touching the pane and feeling that great vibration and wishing for something better. We sat in silence again, and, not knowing what to do, I took her hands and kissed each of them. She smiled and stroked my cheek then smiled more – a great big white crescent of a smile.

Suddenly and from nowhere there was a loud knock on the door and Win yelled out at me, "You done in there, big boy? Come on man, the clock she's a-ticking! Let's go!" It startled the hell out of me but the woman seemed not to notice.

I looked up again at my island woman not knowing her name and not needing to know at this point, really. As she sat on the bed, I rose and bent down, took and kissed her hands again, and, knowing that good sentiments and deeds aren't worth shit in this depraved world, gave her fifty Euros I could ill afford to spend. She rose and kissed me on the cheek and I left without saying a word into the waiting grasp of Win.

"So how was it buddy?" Win punched me in the ribs teasingly. "Man, whooOOO!" Win let out a preternaturally earsplitting *woot* in the tiny hallway that left my ears ringing for quite some time.

"It was great," I told him earnestly and straight-faced. "It was just fine." And I meant it, not that he would understand that special moment.

We walked out the narrow door into clear sunny perfect daylight and again I felt a thousand eyes on me.

"Man that was great," Win exclaimed and then threw his long arm around me. "Aunt Jemima with syrup on top! Hell yeah!" and he gave another tremendous *woot* that echoed through the relatively quiet canal streets. We walked down a side street alongside a pretty canal, avoiding mobs of curious camera wielding tourists, shifty dealers peddling street drugs on canal bridges and the occasional exasperated bicycling local trying to make their slow leaden way through it all.

"Man that fat bitch was great, way better than she looked, and she really knew her shit, man, I tell you," Win rattled off with customary intensity. He went on about orifices and openings and oral this and that and I tuned him out. I suddenly and desperately wanted to be alone, or at least away from Win.

"Say, Win," I interrupted his retelling of his exploits, "I need to do a bit of research, you know, for the book. I gotta go down to see some church museum in the attic of a house. You interested?" I asked knowing this would instantly banish him and he knew it as well.

"No man, you go. I gotta go see about this Indonesian or some such chick I saw in a window before. Man she was smoking hot, just the tightest little hard body you ever seen." He paused and looked wildly around him. "I'll go do that. You go to your little attic church."

I smiled. "You have fun and be safe. See you back at the hotel if not sooner," not really meaning it, but only wanting to get away and be alone.

And we split off, he taking giant strides with his long legs and disappearing into the street crowd, and I turned down the first street I saw, not caring where it took me as long as it was away from here.

I walked forever, taking in the general back-alley vice-ridden graffiti ambiance of some of the Red Light District side streets, then, as the neighborhood turned nicer, the canals and manicured tiny front gardens of more tony streets. Everywhere there were curious lookie-loos, serious agenda-faced young men, giggling teenagers high on weed and locals on black tank bikes barreling through them all. I worked my way out of the Red Light into some other much nicer neighborhood, with more tiny gardens and I saw at the fork of a large canal into two smaller canals, at a great wooden lock, some ancient building half leaning over with a lovely restaurant terrace kissed by the soft northern sun. I resolved to have a bite to eat there and a beer and made my way towards it, circuitously around two bridges. It would have been closer to hop from boat to boat and hopscotch across the canals and if Win had been here he probably would have done it.

I finally arrived and a tall blonde good-looking Dutch bartender that looked a lot like Win, actually, asked me what I wanted to eat and I told him, "Anything." He suggested a sandwich and another twin of a bartender sitting off to the side thumbing through an actual record collection said casually, "No sandwiches left," without looking up.

"Anything man," I insisted, "I'm starving, I'll just have a wheat beer," which is like drinking a loaf of bread. The bartender offered a selection of Fried Dutch Things – his words – and I took him up on it.

I settled outside alone at a table with my wheat beer under that forgiving sun and looked at the boats go by and drained my beer. The food came and it was good: fried cheese, some other yet to be identified thing, also fried, and a croquette of some sort, *bitterballen* I think they called it, fried as well, and I ate it all greedily and thankfully. It soaked up the beer in my belly. I ordered another beer and continued eating. The sun was perfect and all around me was beauty and people and tourists on long tourist canal boats and locals on every imaginable and conceivable permutation of boat, rowboat, raft, skiff, and barge, lazing their happy drunken way past me. They looked so happy, those locals in their small boats with their friends and family. I wanted to drop down onto one from the bridge and join the party, but my act of joyous piracy would probably end in disaster or arrest. It was just about perfect out on that terrace right then and it put me in a great mood and I sat there quietly while drinking it all in.

I moved on reluctantly, and only because my pen ran dry of ink. In the solitude and calm, I had been furiously jotting notes on the Old Church for my Christian guidebook, which was, after all, footing the bill for this adventure. I concentrated on my impressions of the Old Church and tried to put the time with the hookers out of my mind. But with the ink dry, I had little choice but to move on from that restful place.

I ran around a dozen shops meaning to buy a replacement cartridge for my favorite pen. It was hopeless, as store hours had grown alarmingly short during this intensely gorgeous good weather. I finally settled for a plastic pen from a tourist shop selling tiny wooden clogs, hash pipes, tulip bulbs, real and otherwise, and a plethora of other made-in-China knick knacks, including my new bright red pen. It was festooned with the XXX of Amsterdam, which, research proved to me later, was not a porn movie rating at all, but, according to legend, stood for the fire, flood and plague that have periodically decimated the city, or also three Saint Andrew's Crosses representing I don't remember which three saints. But it did not stand for porn movies, no matter what all the tourists coming to the city did to reinforce that mistaken image.

I was hungry again, despite the snack of Fried Dutch Things, and dinnertime was not far away. I did not want to repeat the late dinner fiasco of the previous night, and wanted to eat soon and well. I walked back towards the general area of the hotel, which took me straight into the Red Light District again. As luck would have it, or some fated path of inevitability, Win appeared out of the crowd, looking more and more Dutch with his curly mop of blonde hair and long lithe body. He waved at me and we met on the middle of a bridge, a thousand people and bikes and the occasional doomed car trying to make its way through going around us.

"Hey man, whatcha been doing?" Win asked and didn't wait for an answer. "I just found the hottest, *hottest*, little Filipino girl, good fuck she's smokin' hot, little cutie nice little firm tits good fuck! You gotta come see her you gotta come over," and Win grabbed my hand and led me up the street past *All Movies Ten Euros* and *BDSM Everything Here* and other really nice looking blondes in red neon ringed windows. I shook loose of his grip momentarily.

"Win, man, let's get something to eat. I'm hungry as hell and craving a steak or something substantial."

He nodded, "Okay, okay, I get it. Need more energy for the night ahead, got it," he said and just like that he had forgotten about the hooker and we were looking for food not sex.

We passed a dozen restaurants with Arab man-hawks perched at their entrance. The general decrepitude of the neighborhood, the trash on the ground and the sense of depravities untold lurking and hiding beyond the thin façade of these ancient houses gave the air a tainted and generally unappetizing flavor. Only the hardiest of food could withstand the sex-laden air.

"Let's get some sushi. I've got a hankering for some sushi!" Win said exuberantly and suddenly.

"You poor fuck you, you'd die if you ate sushi here," I told him in no uncertain terms. "The very air is poison here. It would taint that before you even digested it. Only something fried deep and long will do. Better yet, let's get the fuck out of here."

This actually made sense and registered with Win, and we made our way out of the Red Light into a cleaner area of town near Spui, where fresh clean North Sea breezes brought sweet briny air to our noses. It was like being at sea. We sat at an outdoor café at a large intersection and silently watched the bikes and people go by, draining beer after beer, and downing some *bitterballen*, Win eyeing the pretty waitress the whole time, silently imagining untold scenarios with her I'm sure. We finally went back to the hotel to freshen up. The clerk eyed us suspiciously even though we had done nothing wrong yet that I knew about. Maybe he had precognition, or maybe he knew our type. Either way, we freshened up and headed out, with new clothes and a happy reach-to-the-sky attitude, thankful to be in Amsterdam on such a glorious and perfect night.

5

HE PUT HIS BOOTS ON

We eyed a few places to eat a serious meal and Win told me we had best hurry, as we had a date at eight with those girls from Atlanta, and he needed to go back to that Filipino chick tonight at some point.

"Whatever we're going to eat, make it quick," he said restlessly.

We slipped into a nearby dark cozy place plastered with movie posters and lit with dim golden light. We sat next to an American couple who were practically mute the entire time, as if afraid of us. Maybe they were. Win, for his part, was uncharacteristically quiet, eating all my fries – the man lived on fries alone it seemed – and gulping down the tiny beers in one or two swallows.

"What the fuck we doing here?" he asked in a low hoarse voice. "And by we, I mean you, cause I already know I need to get going for those Atlanta girls. And that Filipino bitch too." He eyed me intently with slate grey eyes, and with some menace, I noticed.

"I'm eating, is what I'm doing," I munched on a fry. "What's the hurry, anyway?"

"Eight. I don't want to be late. These girls, and that Monica in particular, are perfect for me. She looks to be naïve as hell, right off the boat," he said, his gaze sinking into me. I squirmed.

"Well, then, let's finish up, have a beer on the way, and get going," I said.

I paid and we left the restaurant, walking fast through long lonely streets populated only by the glow of televisions from apartments above and quiet reddish neighborhood bars containing three or four patrons at most.

"Bar," I said, as we walked by yet another.

"Girls," Win said. "Let's go man, we've got those two belles to attend to." Win walked on ahead of me, pulling me along in his wake.

"I thought we were going for more drinks," I protested. Win ignored me.

We were walking fast now. I was nicely buzzed from the beers at the restaurant, and wanted nothing more than to slow down, have another drink, and keep the buzz going. Win strode along on his long legs, though, as if pulled by some great magnet, going faster and faster as I struggled to keep up.

"Where the hell we going?" I asked. We were working our way back up Damrak towards Centraal Station.

"Those two cuties, man, Monica and Jessica, man. They're up at the," Win brought out a scrap of paper from his pocket, "the NH Palace up there by the train station and we have to meet them at exactly eight o'clock in the P.M. and it's past that now, so we gotta step on it."

The road seemed to stretch on infinitely in front of me. My legs were moving, and moving fast, but I did not feel them. I felt strange, disconnected, like a great big water balloon was sloshing around inside me. Win strode on, oblivious to me, starting to leave me behind.

We crossed the busy street, almost getting run over by maniacal taxis. Finally, the NH Palace loomed ahead.

Win walked into the lobby first, craning his neck around looking for the girls. I was out of breath and sat down in an uncomfortable but stylish chair in the large modern lobby of the hotel. Win spotted Monica and homed in on her. I rose and followed like a long shadow, close, but at a distance, feeling stretched out and wrong.

"Monica!" Win called out, "Hey sorry I'm late but things happened and they were beyond my or any other's control and whatnot and time was playing tricks on us but I'm here and raring to go, so where's your friend?"

"Oh, she was tired of waiting and was pretty exhausted from the trip, anyway," Monica said in a charming southern twang. "But I'm ready to go." She said this with a pert cheerleader smile.

"Fantastic," Win said. "First things first: we must get drink and smoke as soon as possible then we'll start from there."

Win and Monica strode out of the lobby and I followed along, a hapless third wheel. They walked and chatted and Win joked and Monica laughed, and I was invisible. He charmed her, as was his strange gift, something I could never do.

We crossed the Damrak and ended up at The Doors Coffeeshop. The place was crowded, but Win muscled his way in and got a table in the back and he and Monica sat down. I followed but the table was tiny and I ended up standing there. The air was thick and smoky, but pleasantly so, and the music loud.

"*Keep your eyes on the road and your hands upon the wheel,*" counseled Jim Morrison. My hands were definitely off the wheel at that point, and I started to get dizzy. I tried to stand there and enjoy the place, but my head was starting to swim in earnest now. I made my way to the bar and got a pear soda, which I sucked down greedily like an insect, letting its sugary goodness revive me.

Back at the table, Win was rolling what was a very large joint and he lit it, taking several puffs, and passed it to Monica, who took a big drag on it. She held it for a moment, then spurted smoke out her nose and mouth, coughing up a storm. Win laughed and I felt bad for her and offered what was left of my pear soda, but she did not take it. She handed me the joint and I puffed on it. The guy behind her got up and left and I took his seat, sitting there, a voyeur to what was now Monica and Win's date.

I could barely hear them above the music, which was apparently exclusively all Doors material. Dead Jim Morrison sang from beyond the grave. "*The killer awoke before dawn. He put his boots on,*" Morrison warned. Early riser this killer, I thought.

Win gave a tremendous laugh at some joke he'd made and Monica giggled. He looked at me over Monica's shoulder and winked. It really was so very easy for him. This one was no challenge at all.

I drained the last of my pear soda and rose for more fruit juice, as there was no booze in the place. I came back to the table and Win was fishing something out of his pocket. He brought out a little plastic bag and picked a small white pill from it and gave it to Monica. I handed her a pear soda and leaned in closer.

"Don't take candy from a stranger," I said to her. Win shot me an unmistakable "fuck you" look, then turned to Monica and flashed a huge smile.

"And there ain't no one stranger than me," he said and laughed, then Monica laughed.

She took the pill in her hand, looked at it a second, and ate it. Amazing what people will ingest without a second thought.

"Aren't you taking one?" Monica asked Win.

"I took mine already," he said, "so hurry up and catch up to me."

"Is it good?" she asked, tilting her head.

Win leaned in closer to her and brought up his big hand, stroking the side of her head, bringing up a stray lock and tucking it behind her ear. His fingers trailed along her neck.

"Oh, it's gonna be real good, baby," Win almost whispered to her.

I rolled my eyes and looked away. It was getting time for me to get out of there. Check please. The rickety third wheel was falling off.

I scooted further away, sat back and took in the place, ignoring them and waiting for my head to clear. Doors memorabilia plastered the walls top to bottom. Above us, Jim Morrison stood, bare-chested and prophetic, looking down on us with sultry sex-glazed eyes. *Riders on the Storm* played now. The lights dimmed and reddened, throwing a gloomy and menacing vibe over the place. I started getting paranoid, the weed hitting me hard, and I imagined hungry foreign eyes boring into me. The wolves howled and bayed outside.

Meanwhile, Win sat and sweet-talked young Monica. She was doomed. Unable to resist Win's charm. He would have her in any way his twisted mind desired tonight, of that I was sure.

I took one more drag on the joint and stood up dizzily and announced my leaving to anyone that would listen. The two were oblivious to me. I walked out, stumbling through the coffeeshop, taking the joint and spilling out into the cold night air. The door to The Doors closed, leaving the plaintive wails of Jim Morrison behind and Monica to whatever fate she had in store with Win.

The night was beautiful and cool. The street was suddenly silent and peaceful after the manic music and din inside the coffeeshop. I was dizzy and took a moment to settle my vision. I walked forward, hoping to point myself back in the direction of the hotel. I felt strange, disconnected, like the further and further I walked the further I was stretched out, getting thinner and thinner until I was nothing but a filament vibrating crazily in the cool night air. I willed myself on, feeling like I would break, but beyond caring.

I walked on, stretching but somehow not breaking. I skirted the Herengracht in the clear night; the canal beside me was black liquid silver with a constellation of reflected streetlights shimmering on the cold dark surface. Suddenly a large splash rang out in the quiet night. I looked around, immediately paranoid again, but there was no one around, which made it even worse. Soft waves rippled out from the side of the canal, soon reached the other side, and sent a rowboat thumping softly against the canal wall where it was moored.

My head swam again, spinning crazily now, and I leaned against a railing, staring down into the inky water. The long days and nights and the drugs and booze where catching up to me, slowing me down, threatening to take me down. Unseen wolves snarled, prowling around every street corner, closing in. A line from a book I'd read once came seeping darkly into my mind.

I saw a windmill turning death this way.

My grip on the canal railing slipped and I fell to my knees. My vision of the street stretched out to infinity, and a dark tunnel beckoned me, welcoming me into its velvety blackness. I fell forward, catching myself at the last second, having almost fallen into the canal.

I lay on the ground at the edge of the canal looking at the inky blackness below, staring at my face, distorted and wavering in the rippling water. A feeling that something was very wrong crept over me, washing coldly through and around me like the frigid ink of the canal.

An icy darkness swept above me as I sank through the dissolving sidewalk. Over me, wolves closed, snarling and howling. The sidewalk became soft and comfortable, a giant pillow urging me to sleep. I did, yielding and letting darkness engulf me.

6
VEGETABLE MATTER

That next foul morning I woke up, wrecked and with a pounding headache, sitting on a park bench at the edge of the canal. I rubbed my eyes and shivered, chilled to the bone, and made my way back to the hotel through grey cold dawn streets just beginning to wake. Bleary-eyed tourists still slept in hotels and hostels everywhere. Well-dressed young suited businessmen sped by on their black bicycles, and slim tall Dutch women in a kaleidoscope of outfits sped this way and that, some riding two to a bike, one sidesaddle. Municipal workers were out working, sweeping and washing away the debaucheries and detritus of the previous night.

I needed desperately to sit and regroup, warm myself and clean myself up. I ducked into a tiny open breakfast joint at which two large burly working types sat drinking coffee, and I sat at a long low bar, an ancient slab of felled tree which butted up against the big picture window. It was toasty and cozy warm in there – *gezellig* is the word the Dutch use. The fellow behind the counter was friendly and fixed a most delicious simple breakfast with good coffee. I sat, letting the coffee warm me from the inside, and watched the bicyclists outside as I slowly returned to life. I started feeling myself again and although I was exhausted and shaken from the strangeness last night, the strong coffee did its trick and I was wide awake, for the moment.

I desperately needed to get back to the hotel and change and maybe even burn these clothes or, failing that, drown them in some mucky canal. I was sure the wolves could smell them from miles away and maybe fording some water was what I needed to do to throw them off my scent a little longer. I finished my coffee and croissant and left, thanking the cook.

I walked into the hotel and asked for my key, as Win had taken mine, and the clerk gave it to me and gave me a strange look along with it. I made my way up the stairs, not bothering with the slow elevator. I shuffled down the hall to my room, 315, opened the door, and a blast of arctic air and darkness shot out at me. Shivering, I walked in and turned on the lights.

Win was not there, but he had been there. Evidence of corruption littered the trashed room. My heart leapt and I quickly put the "Do Not Disturb" sign on the door, as the maid would not know what to make of this scene and would surely turn us in to hotel personnel, or worse. Bedsheets lay strewn on the ground in clumps and all paintings had been hung facing the walls. All of the furniture lay stacked on one side of the room making a sort of fort and a dog leash and a collar lay neatly coiled up in another corner. Spray from beer or some beverage or liquid ruined the walls and all electrical things were unplugged. The only upright table was covered with beer and soda cans and bottles of every sort, some of which I recognized from the minibar of the first hotel.

I noticed a U.S. passport underneath all the bottles. I looked at it, figuring it was Win's, but it read "Monica Wilma Schaffer" and had a very recent picture of the pretty American blonde from the night before. I turned the new still crisp passport in my hands for some time looking from side to side around the room when suddenly and without warning the door swung wildly open and Win fell inside, shutting it with a slam behind him. He leaned his back against it as if holding it in place, panting hard.

As I caught my own breath from the shock and before I could say anything, Win flapped his lips and shook his head.

"Whew. Fuck. There you are. I've been looking everyfuckingwhere for you dude. I thought you'd be at the bottom of a canal by now."

I rubbed my eyes. The last thing I wanted now was to deal with Win, or this room, or any of his stories. All I wanted was to crawl into some warm bed and sleep all day. To recharge. I wanted to yell at him, tell him to fix up the room and leave, but all that came out was, "What the fuck happened in here?" I looked around the room waving my arms like an idiot.

Win shrugged his shoulders and looked sheepish and innocent, a look that worked well on the ladies but was lost on me.

"Nothing man," he said, eyes cast down, "I mean, I don't know, I was out looking for you, looking out for you, you know, okay?"

"Bullshit, man," I yelled. "Bull-shit. Look at all this shit, man, we gotta get this back together, dude. I can't afford this level of mayhem!"

"Relax man, the room's in my name and besides, we got days left so chill out and by the way, I wasn't here," he said this slowly and came right up on my face, adding, "So chill the fuck out." He said these last words all in my face, poking his hard finger into my chest. He loomed over me, that tall fucker, looking strange and aggressive.

"Fuck it," I raised my hands in exasperation. "Fuck it and fuck you. I need to get out." The wolves were close and I could smell their matted wet death fur. I grabbed a change of clothes from my suitcase buried under twenty towels in the armoire and walked out.

"Just leave," Win said as I walked out, "don't face me, just turn around and ignore me like you ignore everything else!" He stood at the door and continued yelling at me as I hurried down the stairs with a bundle of clothes in my arms. Our lover's spat. "You'll be back," he hollered, then, as I rounded another flight of stairs, added, "And where the hell is Monica? What did you do with her?"

There was true questioning in his voice. I paused a step, my vision and head going light for a second, then kept marching out of the hotel, through the lobby and through the strange worried look of the front desk clerk.

I walked through still waking city streets, skirting Damrak, and walked north to Centraal Station. I needed to get out of town, decompress, regroup. The urge to leave, to flee, was immediate. I changed in the train station bathroom and threw the old clothes in the river behind the station when no one was looking.

Feeling like a new man with new clothes, I went back to the train station and bought a ticket to the first town that came up – some town

I'd never heard of – and hopped on the train. In minutes, I was silently pulling out of Amsterdam into a flat green cow-strewn countryside.

I dozed. Blurry green painted fields, flat as pancakes, greeted my sleepy half-open eyes. I rested and slept, until I came to my stop.

I exited onto a maze of escalators and people. Proclaimed announcements in Dutch, all gibberish to me, filled the air. I raced through the station and hopped on another train. I was the last one on, barely making the connection, and settled in for another ride and more cows and countryside.

Tiny greenhouses and thatched roof barns appeared solemnly on the flat green sea of grass. Canals higher than the surrounding land were kept dangerously and nervously at bay by polders. Then, the land turned to deep forest with trees growing diagonally as if some unseen wind was blowing them over, or as if all of creation itself was tilted off kilter. The trees straightened and dark boughs of unseen damp forests beckoned with mystery and solitude and danger.

The train stopped at some tiny town and only I and a couple of locals got off, the parents waiting on the platform and embracing long-absent backpacked youths. I walked past them and out the station and sat under a tree on a little hill and inhaled the rich cow manure clean country air. My ears were assaulted by the silence. The solitude and distance were doing me good, erasing the debaucheries of the previous nights. The wolves were far. I had eluded them – for now.

I napped like Newton under the tree and a bus pulled in and woke me up. I decided to hop aboard. A group of eighteen lost Greek tourists appeared from nowhere and scrambled on board after me and the bus shut its doors and moved on. I eyed the Greeks warily. Had they followed me? Had the wolves sent them? The bus stopped in the middle of nowhere and I got off and crossed the road. The Greek phalanx exited as well and followed me, but they seemed hapless and lost and not wolflike in the least so I relaxed a little.

It started to rain then and I ducked under a tiny tree, literally ducked, in a small but beautifully manicured garden. A beat to shit old

Peugot pulled in the driveway and even before she got out I saw her. A stunner. Tan smooth summer beach skin, gorgeous model-perfect face framed by hair which clung to her like spun gold, or rays of light coalesced into fleeting flowing beautiful solid energy. She caught me looking and I could not politely look away but had to stare, my parched dry eyes drinking in quenching life water. I stared looking like what I was: a wet lunatic crouching under her tree or – at best – some hapless mental idiot in need of special care. I did not care, though, and I tried to force my slack jawed gaping mouth into something resembling a smile, but it came off funny and she darted in the door.

A minute later she came out with her lithe swimmer boyfriend and they ran through the rain and hopped in the car and were off again, both eyeing me warily. I stared at her golden hair as she drove away until it was only a star of light in the distance. I had a sudden and crazy urge to break into her house and wait for her and pledge my undying love and fealty for her, but it was a silly and dangerous plan and I dismissed it.

Another bus pulled up and I got on if only to get out of the rain, and the eighteen Greeks followed me on board. I grabbed a seat and we all traveled silently for some time, the locals on the bus doing their daily crosswords and wondering about this Greek invasion and naturally assuming I was one of them.

The bus stopped and I got off and the Greeks got off and I darted across the street, going away from them, and I walked down quiet misty country roads. The silence between the occasional passing cars was amazing and beautiful and I welcomed it like a long lost friend. I passed large houses with gorgeous flowered cared-for lawns, a field of large black and white healthy cows, and trees that lined the road and sheltered me from most of the light rain coming down.

I got to the end of the road and was at a huge national park, the Hoge Veluwe, which I'd always wanted to see and fortune or providence or subconscious thought had brought me to. I knew, from my research for my increasingly doomed Christian guidebook, that in the middle of the sprawling park was the Kröller-Müller museum, one of the biggest and best in the country, which is inexplicably tucked away from absolutely everything and very difficult for a tourist to reach. Only dogged determination or idiot luck brings one here. Filled with the latter, I went to the ticket booth, paid to get in and grabbed a white bike available to anyone to use for free from a big bike corral at the front. Here in this communist Schwinn enclave, all shared freely of these bikes. I hopped on the bike and – *good crap it's been a long, long time since I've ridden* – I set off yawing crazily like an epileptic drunk. I soon found my groove, though, and pedaled through dark forests that opened up into foreign flatlands of polders and tiny purple flowers and it was wide open and no one was around and the wind rushed past me and I gave a great giggling schoolboy laugh at the wonder and majesty of it all.

I desperately wanted to find some quiet and forgotten copse and hide my bike and just sleep forever under welcoming sheltering trees, but it was still raining lightly and picking up and turning cooler. I saw a sign for the museum and bent my crazy white bike towards it and a kilometer and a half disappeared under the splendor of woods and nature. I parked my communist bike, really only left it as I would most likely pick up a different one later, and it felt strange and liberating to not own or be responsible for this bike and to not fear its theft.

I walked into the museum and immediately made a beeline for some coffee. I sat in the café for a while drinking the rich brew, drying off and warming myself.

Then, to my total non-surprise, in the door walked the eighteen Greek tourists, making it here by sheer determination alone. I eyed them warily but they still felt harmless and I think it was only happenstance that brought us together. I finished the rest of my coffee and, rested, cleaned up and relaxed, I made my way to the museum proper.

An embarrassment of riches greeted me here in the middle of these woods. Van Goghs without number hung in amazing living color testimony to the man who had painted them. I sat and stared at them transfixed for what seemed like hours, staring in particular at a painting of an arrangement of flowers seemingly captured by some witch doctor voodoo magic or perhaps some divine gift, their very life and texture thickly painted on canvas to freeze them fresh and in beauty for eternity. People walked around me and probably thought I was stoned or tripping, but I was stone cold sober and just enjoying this magic, which grew the more you looked at it. Harried tourists gave it cursory three second glances and hurried off to the next, seeing everything and nothing. The Greeks were there, and I hoped at least one of them found meaning and beauty and a respite from cold icepick realities here in this beauty-filled and secret place, as I did. I breathed in and closed my eyes and the flowers remained bright and vivid in front of me and for a moment I was far away from myself and everything was right and nothing was wrong.

Right after that tiny magic moment was when it all went wrong.

I wandered around outside in an awesome sculpture garden viewing things odd and beautiful and incomprehensible. A giant stylized duck was propelled by the wind on a small lake. Upon closer inspection it was only geometric figures that from a distance resembled a duck. One sculpture allowed me to enter it through a tiny nautical seashell entrance and climb my way to its insane top where I stood on a black and white relief map of an alien world. I wandered into another sculpture, which wasn't really a sculpture in the traditional sense, but strange music emanating from the very earth, creating an incredible surreal stereophonic sensation with nothing but trees around. I examined the trees for speakers but there were none, and the music was coming straight out of the ground. I sat on the earth for a time and felt the vibrations and wondered about the artist and what possessed them to do this and how it was even possible. I reclined on the cool grass and closed my eyes for a minute and was instantly in a deep, lovely sleep in some mystical world, but not for long. It started to drizzle and I woke up and got up and shivered, putting my hands in my pockets to warm myself.

That's when I felt a strange non-wallet, non-coin thing in my pocket, like a little balled up piece of chewing gum wrapped around a napkin. I fished out a crumpled napkin, which I unfolded to reveal a small grey lump of some vegetable matter. On the napkin, in Win's huge and distinctive writing, was the word "EAT." I sat back down on the ground feeling the surreal vibrations and looking at the little grey lump, smelling it. It smelled of cut salad mushrooms and looked evil and moldy, like a hardened piece of blue cheese. I wondered what the hell this was and for a strange second I could have sworn I saw Win behind the tree magically whispering in my ear, *"Do it you scared fucker do it already,"* and then, on impulse, I popped the whole thing into my mouth.

I bit it and it crumbled apart in my mouth and it did taste rather like a fresh salad mushroom. I chewed it but was afraid to swallow, but errant bits got through and slid down my throat and it starting changing flavors, turning to bitter herbs then to acidic bile. I wanted desperately to spit it out but there were respectable looking folk everywhere and it was, after all, a sculpture garden, an art exhibit of some renown. My ill-advised cow cud spittle would not have been welcome. I finally made my way to some private trees and spit the vile wretched stomach juice mushroom out of my mouth. I brought out my water bottle to rinse and was dismayed to find it empty. I quickly went back to the museum proper and rapidly to the bathroom where I waited to be alone then rinsed my mouth out with cool water that did nothing to get rid of the acid taste. I really wanted something, anything, to eat but I had a certain feeling that anything I put in my mouth would be returned to sender in right quick step. I took small sips of water, cursed at Win for poisoning me, cursed myself for listening to him, and cursed the bile toad living in my mouth.

I left the bathroom and felt wired like I had just mainlined a double shot of espresso. All traces of my previous exhaustion were gone, and, other than my mouth, I felt great. I had wanted to look at the Van Gogh flowers one last time but now they looked flat and amateurish. I desperately needed to be outside. Only real flowers would do now. I soon was, and I picked another bike out of the available racks. This one was a winner, nice taut tires and greased chain, a class ride proving that there was no equality in this communist bike utopia. The bike launched forward with a seeming will of its own and soon I was rushing through sunlight dappled forest lanes past pensioners and little kids weaving like drunks on the trail, which opened up into that amazing open savannah, like a seagrass strewn beach without an ocean. For all I knew, that is what it was. I pedaled furiously and yelled in the air praises to the Creator for this wonder before me and I felt absolutely great, like I could pedal forever on this sturdy bike.

The trail wound its long lonely way through more and more grassland and, suddenly and without warning, I felt like I was running out of steam. *Just because you feel okay doesn't mean you are okay,* I remember thinking to myself, and I began to turn around, but then saw the end of the grasslands and beginning of some dark forest which I had a sudden urge and need to get to.

I rode on at a slower saner pace, trying to reserve enough energy for the ride home. I arrived at the edge. It was a dark primeval Robin Hood forest with ancient friendly trees and it was cool and inviting without that sense of foreboding sometimes found in dark forests such as this one. In a short while, I came to a fork in the path and a mile – or kilometer, I suppose – marker listing various distances, including five plus kilometers back to where I needed to return. I stopped and hesitated for a while and caught my breath and decided I had to press on at least a little longer to see what was down either of these paths. Frost would have had a field day with me if I didn't travel down at least one of these roads. I looked down one as far as I could, to where it bent in the undergrowth, Frost's ghost waving at me. Down I went, my bike leaping at my touch like a well-trained seal gunning for a fish.

In no time I came across a most beautiful lake with a large mansion in the distance, the reflection doubling the whole scene for a twice as beautiful experience. Low grey wispy clouds fragmented and let the blue sky behind them stray through and it was insanely gorgeous and indescribable. I pulled in to a picnic area in front of the lake as a young woman helped an old frail lady out of her car and they made their slow cane-walking shuffling way over to a bench by the lake. I sat on a far bench, leaving the one with the better view for them but they ended up sitting on the bench closest to them and the good and perfect view went unoccupied. Granddaughter and grandmother, I assumed, sat tenderly and peacefully and hugged and looked at the lake and did not say much. It was touching and I reclined on the bench and looked up at the yellow green fluttering leaves just beginning to change color. I forgot my troubles and insanity and wished the best for that dear old grandmother and her daughter, and when I got up, which did not feel like very long, they were both gone and I sensed a presence there, something like a holy place where they had been. I wanted to build an altar right at the spot but no crude construction of sticks and rocks could capture the love and tenderness of that moment, so fleeting, and, I sensed, so final and last.

I reclined back and shut my eyes. Darkness, then a deeper darkness, came over me and the pale summer sun had been blotted out by dark grey lead skies. I arose and my legs felt weak and disconnected from my body and my belly and midsection felt curious and distant to my touch. *That fucker Win.* Whatever he had given me was now kicking in earnestly and I still had to negotiate bikes and buses and changes and trains and much walking just to get back to the hotel. I considered calling a cab, but how would I do that here in the middle of a forest, and how would I pay for it? It was folly. Lethally expensive. Instead, I willed my legs to move and I walked forward, with my head following shortly thereafter. I prayed I looked more normal than I felt, hoped I was not doing some Groucho Marx legs-forward strange lumber through the woods. They would shoot me and mount my hide in some rich hunting lodge somewhere.

I got to my bike without seeming incident or attention and was soon on it, steady, and rolling forward, letting momentum and immutable physics take hold. Forward, forward back from whence I came, I pedaled on, passing families and impulsively sticking my tongue out at a kid who was six or so and pedaling his damnedest with his tiny little legs trying to keep up. Some septuagenarian in front of me stopped, wobbled and toppled over in slow motion. I stopped and asked him and his wife if he was alright and the words came out strange and I hope I had said them right, but the only injury seemed to be to his pride, though he did have a Band-Aid on his elbow indicating this may not have been his only fall.

I pedaled, feeling great now, the heaving queasy waves of nausea having wafted harmlessly above me like nerve gas blowing over a trench. My mask held. But then I slowed and felt myself get clammy suddenly. The thought of the ends-of-the-world voyage still ahead of me made me pull over and almost puke out of despair, but I maintained and soon I was back at the bike ranch and my trusted steed was corralled for the night. I got off the bike and suddenly felt very slow and ponderous and I had a desperate aching empty hunger like a black hole in my gut. I needed something in me soon and a kilometer or more of rural emptiness lay between the village and me. I thought back to the small herring stand I had seen at the crossroads of town where the bus had dropped me off and how I'd always wanted one of those herrings – the Dutch version of sushi – and here was my chance for that delicious pickled fish.

I walked on resolute and serious and on a mission for food. Then, I must have started hallucinating. I saw a forlorn teenage boy riding with what must have surely been his sad father on a tiny wagon, being pulled by a miniscule horse the size of a German Shepherd, all being led by a pale-faced freckled short Dutch girl in some strange and tattered period costume. To top off the surreal scene, a small black dog sat in the miniature coach as the driver in his little driver's seat. I suddenly and strongly felt an irresistible wave of laughter at this surreal tableau before me, and I knew without doubt that if I started laughing it would be raucous, socially inappropriate and would devolve into maniacal cackling that I would be unable to stop, perhaps ever.

I walked by. I was walking as slow as can be and was still faster than this sad toy horse and its strange load and I could not stop staring. The girl in costume looked at me and I looked away then looked back and I said, "That's a tiny, tiny horse," then gave one short cackle which I hoped sounded like a cough, and the girl gave me a big Pippi Longstocking smile and I screwed up my face and tried urgently not to laugh. I knew if I began it would be the end of me. Butterfly nets and padded rooms. Instead I looked at the sad pitiful awkward teenager and his sullen-faced dad sitting facing away from each other, distant, and tried to figure out their story. Was this some strange village idiot punishment of humiliation, some backwards custom of this small town? Perhaps, but probably not. The dad had that distinctly out-of-touch-with-reality look; he seemed clueless to the fact that hayrides on tiny horse drawn carts are the stuff of six year olds, not a boy of surely fourteen or more. What strange and twisted set of events led to this Fellini film scene before me? Was I hallucinating? Maybe. I took out my camera and played the dumb tourist card and snapped a picture of what I hoped would not be empty air later. Though, thinking about it, a hallucination would be easier to explain.

I walked faster past that crazy cart, laughter stalking me the whole way, and came to the village crossroads. Finally, food. But one look at the herring stand and waves of revulsion swept through me. I ducked into a grocery store for some chocolate, which sounded like just the ticket. I looked around and I was having trouble focusing on the items. Everything was just happy mushroom colors and I could not distinguish items very well and my eyes were watering. The feeling soon subsided and I realized I was in some sort of department hardware dollar store and went right back out across the street to the real grocery store.

I looked around, trying to focus, and finally grabbed a huge bar of chocolate and stood in line behind a little kid. The kid was buying chocolate also and he put a little separator bar between his chocolate trove and my candy bar and then for good measure a separator between my candy bar and the person behind me. I marveled at the conscientiousness of the kid, which contrasted horribly with my own kill-or-be-killed American Wild West mentality.

The line moved at a snail's pace. I had to really control the impulse to tear into my chocolate bar like a rabid dog. I eyed the purchases of my young *compadre* in front of me and he seemed to have scored infinitely better candy on his trip through the store. The lady behind me also had some good looking fine chocolates in her purchases, and I wondered if "they" were secretly keeping all the good candy for themselves and letting the tourists have the generics. For a crazy moment I saw myself batting the kid aside and taking all his candy like a giant fairy tale ogre, booming laughter and walking out of the store mighty and triumphant. The clink of coins brought me back to reality and the kid spent his allowance counting out pennies or whatever they used over here for that. Then it was my turn and I quickly paid for mine and had it open before I crossed the outside threshold and was eating it like some degenerate stoner junkie from an early-sixties propaganda film.

I took one bite of the chocolate and knew it was a mistake. It tasted like that damn mushroom still, like a bile toad peeing in my mouth. I wanted to spit the whole thing out but it would be wholly inappropriate here and disgusting brown sludge coming out of my mouth might make me puke for good. I let the chocolate melt in my mouth, took tiny sips from my water bottle, and pointed myself in the direction of the bus stop. I looked at an unintelligible map, saw a crowded stop with nowhere to sit, and went across the road, dejected, to a bus stop on the opposite side, where there was no one waiting and the bench was all mine. What did it matter? All roads led to Amsterdam. It was inevitable and magnetic.

I waited for seeming ever looking for a long time at the maps and routes, my mind not being able to comprehend anything. *Damn you Win*. If he was here at least he could maintain better than I. As it was, I rode waves of nausea and had a sudden and very real fear of getting on the bus, if and when it came, and splattering the windows with vomit or puking into my bag and ruining my meager possessions (which consisted of a water bottle, a journal and XXX pen, a blank journal I'd bought at the museum, and a chocolate bar with one bite taken out).

After waiting for untold time, a cute punk rocker girl with torn black hose and heavy black makeup walked up and sat as far away from me as she could, studiously avoiding even eye contact with me. She was strange and out of place here in this idyllic countryside. Maybe she was going to Amsterdam, in which case she would think that I was following her and denounce me to the police who would take me in for questioning, and who knows what I would say under the influence of whatever drug this was. I tried to clear my mind but visions of gulags kept coming in, so I studied that map some more and that did the trick, my mind unable to do anything but try to make sense of that bus map and compass points that swung around like bobble headed dolls.

After days of waiting the bus came and I boarded after the punk girl. I was unable to be seated until finishing a long English-less discussion with the bus driver who seemed to be demanding payment even though I had a return ticket that I knew I had purchased when I was sober, and I had to buy another ticket and I didn't care because I only wanted to sit down and not vomit. I sullenly paid for another ticket and sat, concentrating every neuron on not hurling. After a bit I relaxed and settled into the seat and watched the scenery unscroll. The driver was a beast, gunning the bus and pushing it fast, and the green leaves hyperspaced and blurred into a thousand mosaics and shades and points of green blue and yellow that looked like someone had spun washed a Seurat. Warp drive green and yellow leaves and trees painted my vision and it was beautiful and majestic I sat there enjoying it.

The bus spat me out in Arnhem and I got out just in time after seeing the little railroad symbol on a construction site. It was indeed a train station behind walls and barricades. I hopped on what I hoped was the right train, my brain feeling more in my control again. Fast telepathic trains and neural networks of people flowed and I tried to plug in and allow myself to be carried and I changed trains by magic and soon I was pulling into Amsterdam Centraal once again.

I wove my way out of the station and through crowded summer streets, ravenously wolf hungry now that I thought I could keep it down. The strangeness had passed and only a slight heady sensation remained. I stopped by a little sandwich shop and got myself a *tosti*, basically a grilled cheese sandwich, but infinitely better. I devoured it right there at the counter getting a raised eyebrow from the cashier, but I did not care. My stomach gurgled, did one flip, but then settled down and the *tosti* was there to stay. Sated for the moment, I finally went back to the hotel.

I got the key from the increasingly suspicious front clerk and ran up to the room going up the stairs two at a time. I came to the door, 315, and opened it expecting that arctic blast and was instead greeted by a misty jungle fog. It was hot as hell in there, like a steam room, and a low steam cloud sat right about eye level. I went in cautiously and the room had changed.

Everywhere there were exotic plants and flowers, tiny orchids, broad-leafed tall plants, bromeliads, and big potted ferns. I looked to my right to the bathroom and the door was open and there sat Win inside the giant tub, filled to the absolute brim, *over* the brim, so that water tension alone kept it from spilling over. Win floated like an alligator, nose barely above the water, the rest of his body submerged in the big tub. I began to say something, to ask him what in God's good green earth was going on, but he slowly rose, lifting his head a bit enough for his mouth to clear the surface, which made the water level drop ever so slightly, and let out a long snakelike "shhhhhhhhh . . ." and I closed my mouth, tilted my head, and didn't know what to think or say. He turned his head ever so slightly to look at me, and his face was strange, pupils totally black and bestial, eyes watering, mouth turned in a big goofy grin with either drool or water or both coming out, and cheeks taut and red like he had been laughing hysterically for hours. He sunk back into the water and the water rose alarmingly and I thought it would spill.

"You've really done it now," I said after a spell, despite his admonishment. "Where the hell did you get all these plants and bushes and why and how did you get them all up here? And this damned tub, dude, do you have any idea how much water weighs? You're gonna go right through the floor!" I had visions of the old timbers giving out and the tub and Win plummeting through three floors, taking out everything beneath him, leaving a perfectly oval cartoon hole in its wake.

Win rose again slowly and in a low alien voice said, "Shhhhhhhhh . . . . You're screwing up the membrane transfer. I am absorbing the water and dispersing myself," and after this strange statement he went back down, nose barely above water, glossy black licorice eyes fixed forward. If he'd had a blowhole he would have submerged completely.

I sighed. There was no way of reaching him now. Best to let whatever held him release its talon grip slowly. I backed out of the bathroom slowly and quietly closed the door, but there was no way of locking or blocking it. I was exhausted but feared sleep, specially here in this jungle. Too many wolf eyes could lurk in the tropical foliage. It was hot as hell in the room, August in Florida hot. I opened the window and a rush of steam escaped and died outside and clean cool air entered and I made a little fortress out of pillows and an upturned ottoman around one of the beds jammed in the corner, curled up and went into a dead quick one-eye-open sleep.

7
BRICK WAVES

I awoke some time later – it could have been hours or Rip Van Winkle years or centuries later. I was groggy but my body felt good, rested. I heard a splash in the bathroom and clicked alert. *Win. The tub.*

"Get out of there you fool, you'll go hypothermic in no time if you haven't already!" I yelled out.

The door opened and a wall of steam burst forth like an old Mississippi river steamboat or some great primeval Yellowstone geyser.

"No chance, buddy," Win said, emerging pink, almost reddish, and wearing only a stark white towel. He was cleaning his ears furiously with a white Q-tip, really getting in there.

"Good fuck you look like a steamed lobster," I said.

"It was the only way to keep them at bay. They intensely dislike tropical climes," he responded, and I did not delve into this paranoid fantasy. It was probably total paranoia induced fantasy fodder and if it wasn't – well, that possibility was even more difficult and frightening to swallow, so I left it alone.

"Get dressed dude, let's get out of this place and grab some breakfast," I said, hunger suddenly consuming me. The room, despite the plants, was somewhat put back into shape, and my anger from before had receded and been swallowed by my drug-induced cosmic trip.

Win was very mellow and uncommonly placid and actually did get dressed and we were soon bounding down the stairs two at a time and out into the misty cool dawn to the same breakfast place I'd eaten at the day before. Good Lord, was that only a day ago? It felt like eons of time had elapsed.

We sat at a tiny table in the tiny place and I ordered a breakfast and Win shook his head but I ordered a croissant and coffee for him in order to safeguard my own. When it came he sat there, picking the flakes off. He did sip at the coffee and came back to life quickly.

"Ooo weee man," he stretched his long arms and gave a tremendous yawn, big enough for a lion tamer to stick his head in. "That was some crazy shit man, did you eat my little gift to you? I did, I ate it, ate about ten times what I gave you and I had to build my own jungle planet, it just had to be done. What a ride, man. I was fuuuucked up, man," then in a huge sonic boom voice, "I ain't ever been that fucked up in a long time."

He fell silent a second as I continued eating greedily before we were kicked out or asked to leave. I took a last bite of the croissant and washed it down with too hot coffee, burning my tongue a little.

"I absolutely and without a doubt have got to get some work done today," I said. The time was running out and I had exactly none of this damned guidebook written. Win waved his hand dismissively.

"Aw, don't worry about it man, you'll get it done, now besides I got big plans for us today."

I shook my head but knew right away that the day was done. It was Win's now and I had to hang on and hope to come out alive and sane and in one piece at the end of it.

"So!" Win punched me on the arm, a small bruise now rising there from inside. "How was it man, you ate it right?"

"Yeah I ate it," and I told him about it, about the museum and the bicycles and the little miniature pony cart and the strange tripping color bus ride. Truthfully, in the cool renewing morning air, I actually was glad that I had eaten that vile mushroom. Once the dead snakeskin vomitous realities had been sloughed off by time and rest, some really cool little mind pictures and experiences remained. Not to mention that riotous tiny ridiculous horse that I would not forget anytime soon. I was at least glad I had experienced it.

"See man," Win punched me in the arm playfully, "I'm looking out for you buddy."

And he was, in his own crazy Win-like way. He was a unique animal but at the end of the day he could get me through the day, though not necessarily in one piece. And probably at the expense of others he'd left in his wake.

"Listen dude," I told him earnestly, "you have got to see some Van Goghs before we leave." I told him about the flower picture. "There's more to this city than drugs and whores you know."

"Boats and hoes boats and hoes, yeah," Win said, far away, tuning me out, in his own world, not listening – still, something had to get through. Maybe the sheer preternatural genius of those paintings would open up his horizons and realities a bit.

"Let's go man, let's go to the museum," I said, trying to muster him while we was still mellow. I needed to hit at least one of the museums in Amsterdam proper for my guidebook. Maybe take notes and try to remember it without Win's shamanic drugs clouding the memories.

"Right, right," Win said, seeming to agree with me for once, and we got up and I paid and we walked out into the increasingly sunny and cool beautiful Amsterdam morning. Bikes and girls and girls on bikes and canal boat tourists and pimply giggling zippy-eyed teens were everywhere and the city reared up and woke. We walked, enjoying it all.

"Hold on, dude," Win said and disappeared down a side street crowded with shoppers. I stood waiting for a while, happy to be watching everything unreel in front of me. Win came back with a little paper bag.

"What's in the bag?" I asked and he smiled devilishly and then grew alarmed and opened his eyes wide.

"Shit!" he yelled out and a couple of heads turned. "We gotta go back to the hotel now!"

"Why?" I asked.

"Forgot to put up the Do Not Disturb. If the maid finds my personal jungle in there, we're cooked."

"Fine, come on," I said. We were a minute from the hotel anyway and soon we were inside the room and everything was as we'd left it, which is to say, a royal mess.

"So what's in the bag?" I asked again, sitting down on the edge of the bed.

"For the museum, dude. This – *this* – will blow your mind with your fancy paintings and all," Win said producing a little plastic container. He opened it and gave me two small mushrooms, long stalked things with little white bald heads.

"Oh no, nope. Not at all. Nope, had enough yesterday, thanks but no thanks," I told him in no uncertain terms.

"Nah nah, man these are different – totally different – you gotta try these, dude they'll blow your mind," he gave me a big sincere grin, "but not too much," he added after seeing the worried and reluctant look on my face.

I shook my head but Win was persistent and before I knew it I had popped the two mushrooms in my mouth. They tasted totally normal, good even, and nothing like what I had had the previous day. Nothing happened for a long time.

I was about to tell him that nothing was happening and I that was going back outside when I froze, admiring the Persian carpet on the ground, its very interesting and twirling designs, a cogwheel fantasy machine of moving parts and swirls and everything was an intense shade of deep red like the mouth of a furnace was lighting the room. I sat down on the floor right by the rug, transfixed on it, not wanting to step foot in it for fear of getting caught in the gears, and sat there for who knows how long. I turned after a while to look at Win who was staring intently at the brick wall outside our window. He turned his head and it seemed bigger, rounder, like a strange frightening cherubim of old – not flying-baby-with-wings cute cherubim, but more the guarding-gates-to-Eden-with-flaming-swords cherubim, big and unnatural and menacing. I felt the sudden and intense sensation of being watched and looked at the dark wood beamed wooden ceiling as the eyes of a thousand wolves looked back at me from every knot in the wood. They had found me and were here ready to pounce.

I needed to be outside just then, as quick as possible. Out in big open empty spaces with living trees, not around felled cut ones with their knot eyes staring and menacing.

"I need to get out," I said with some effort, it was difficult to speak, and got up unsteadily, legs disobedient and jellylike and unwilling to contribute to propulsion. "I'm going to the park, I gotta get outside, dude," I announced to Win again.

"You'll never make it. The lobsters will get you for sure," he said in an even monotone, still not taking his eyes off the wall.

"I have to. No choice," I said and fished for my wallet, making sure I had it on me – I still had at least that much sense – and I lurched my way over to the door. I cracked it open, and looked out in the hall until no one was coming and somehow made it down the stairs without breaking my neck and past the lobby and out into the intense white bright creation light of the day.

The intensity of it all made me want to scream in joy and terror. I stood on the porch of the hotel, leaning on the black cool sturdy iron railing, and looked at the thin wispy white clouds skirting the sky, adding a layer of creation to the blue and swimming liquid air around me. I was only a fish or other sea creature – *look out for the lobsters!* – making my way down undulating streets, the bricks cresting and falling in waves in this floating city. The air was a thick and palpable miasma of jellied liquid that I could somehow easily and beautifully breathe. Despite my exalted feelings, movement itself was difficult on uncooperative legs.

I left the protective confines of the porch and lurched to small iron posts festooned with the XXX of Amsterdam that lined every street here. I later learned these are called *Amsterdammertjes*, or "little ones from Amsterdam," but right then, they were only posts, and they kept me from falling. I lurched from one to the other like an anesthetized gorilla with a large feathered dart in its ass. I was being hunted and they were close enough to bring me down. I had to speed up, but this only ruined my rhythm and I almost fell into the street after missing one the savior posts, these little ones keeping me upright. A bicycle whizzed past me so fast that it was yards past down the road before I even realized or registered it.

With sheer lunatic will I made it across smaller streets and a good ways down the road until I got to a busy intersection. This was no mere easily negotiable side street, but an honest thoroughfare with bikes and cars and buses and trams thrown in to boot all moving at different speeds. I looked around and the cars sped by in huge multicolored blurs of light and the trams lumbered like death itself, unstoppable. I stood leaning on a lamppost, looking at this frightening Frogger maze and knew it would keep me from the sanity and serenity and safety of the park and I also knew I would be squashed like a frog if I tried to cross, and then it occurred to me that I didn't even know where the park was or where *I* was in relation to it. Defeated, I turned around and made my drugged ape walk back to the hotel, great big waves of sidewalks and bricks cresting and falling in this doomed city adrift on the sea. Its very foundations and existence was laughable and yet inspiring, a testament to dogged insane determination.

I was back at the hotel and muttered something about it being too wavy outside to the flabbergasted clerk. I waited for the elevator for a century then gave up, went up the stairs and by the end was crawling up to our room. I opened the door and the last thing I remember was Win giving a tremendous Samurai yell and long arms and legs coming at me and then darkness swallowed me and did not spit me out for a very long time.

8
NAZI BASTARDS

Darkness, warm and womblike, sheltered me for untold time, voices disembodied and unintelligible circled like far off satellites and pinpoints of stars and dreams washed over me in warm wet waves. In the darkness with eyes wide open I could see nothing but stars and when I brought my hand in front of me there was nothing there at all. The stars blinked and it got warm and they slowly turned into the eyes of wolves, distant, but closing, and I could not hide or shelter myself because there was nothing around me but absence, pure and absolute.

Win's voice whispered then shouted in my head – *Get up, wake up, wake up fucker!* – and I felt gravity pulling on my body. I rolled to the side, rose and cracked my head hard on the bottom of the bathroom sink, a supernova explosion of light discharging in my skull and destroying the galaxies of wolf eyes, and my body dropped from the void. Slowly the bathroom came into focus even as a huge and warm rhythmic thumping started in my head where I had knocked it. The bathroom, formerly a white porcelain spotlessly clean affair, was now a jungle nightmare with potted tropical plants, carnivorous tiny jawed flytraps, ferns, orchids of all types with their beautiful erotic blooms and countless other plants jammed into the place.

With effort I got up and threaded my way around the plants and out of the bathroom. As I did I caught sight of myself in the mirror behind some unidentified plant and jumped, startled at my bestial appearance emphasized all the more by my jungle surroundings. Wild matted hair and scraggly beard, tired dead mineral eyes and a trickle of blood running from my scalp all made me look like some troglodyte prehistoric forest creature not yet evolved to a man. I saw a flash behind me, thought I saw Win's curly blonde hair and spun around to look but there was no one there. I stumbled to the sink, cleared an orchid sitting there and a flower fell off and I washed my face and felt the monkey-mask sloughing off and humanity slowly returning. I wanted to shave but had sworn that I wouldn't until I finished this damned guidebook. I had visions of myself with a huge Moses beard, grandchildren pulling at it and guidebook still unfinished in some dusty corner somewhere, me the victim of some foolish Nazirite vow.

I left the bathroom and entered the main room and it was a mess, though now cleared of plants, all of them having been stuffed into the bathroom. Win was nowhere to be found. The furniture lay arranged amateurishly and without thought or reason and all around was the detritus of travel: expired train and bus tickets, folded up tourist maps creased and useless, change of strange coins in all denominations together with crumpled Monopoly money, receipts from useless things bought and paid for and now forgotten, toiletries from a dozen hotels or more, half-eaten candy bars, a few warm unopened beers and dirty and clean clothes mixed and strewn everywhere and wet underwear hanging from a radiator. I was disgusted by this room and by my general appearance. I needed to get out and I made myself as presentable as possible, changing, combing my mop of hair and walking out the door.

I was back on the streets, hands in pockets on a gorgeous North Sea windy blue-skied day. The very air and sun cleansed me and filled me with humanity again. I had no idea of the time and walked on, glancing at people's wrists until I found a nice big face and I read it was about two o'clock. I walked on and on, up, over and around canals and bridges, just ecstatic at being alive and sober, if still a little dizzy from the huge knot on my head. How long had Win left me in that jungle bathroom? I had no idea of the day even and for all I knew my time here was already done and over and I had scant material for a guidebook of any sort.

I walked through unfamiliar streets and over more bridges and everywhere people buzzed around as if on some enormous circuit board, electric and alive, each a tiny spinning atom as I was and the thought of all this made my head hurt but made me glad and warm as well. I kept an eye out for Win, not concerned for him as much as the denizens and visitors of this fair city. Everywhere there were happy people enjoying one last blast of sun before grim winter ice claws dug in. The wolves were far and I could not even hear their distant moonlight howl.

After untold steps I walked into a small wood-paneled bar for rest and a drink. The place was way the hell off the beaten track and none but locals populated it. They gave me cursory glances upon arriving, but seemed like a friendly lot. The sounds of what I thought was a record or a player piano filled the small cozy bar but it was a wizened old man in a grey woolen cap sitting at an upright piano playing some virtuosic and complicated piece of classical music that I did not know. It was amazing to me. I ordered a beer at the bar from a kindly old woman who poured me a tiny Heineken that was so cold that it hurt a little to drink and I sat down at a large open wooden table. I ordered a selection of Fried Dutch Things and another beer from a waiter a bit later, and soaked in the scene.

Countless posters and pictures of all sorts lined the walls, giving no clue as to the color that lay underneath. A couple of old men sat in a corner and had a heated discussion and they looked like they were lifelong friends and I could picture them having come into this bar since 1945 with not much having changed except their age. Two men played billiards, not pool but billiards, with a red, yellow and white ball, and I watched them for a long time, fascinated at the geometric complexity and forethought necessary to play this on a mental level, to say nothing of the physical coordination necessary to pull it off. The soft click of the billiard balls filled the silence between the piano pieces as the piano master changed the sheet music with soft rustling. When he finished a piece, he would turn around as if expecting applause and indeed he was expecting applause – and deserved it. He did not start playing again until he had been recognized.

The little old man pulled out another booklet of sheet music from a leather satchel he kept on a table beside him, placed the music reverently on the piano like the Host on an altar, smoothed out the pages, got real serious and started playing. Four notes into it I could tell it was Bach. He was following me around Amsterdam as if trying to tell me something, to communicate some sacred truth with me from three hundred years in the past. The notes soared around me, filling the cozy bar with light and joy and I closed my eyes and listened. Everything else fell away and the noise of the billiard balls clinked softer and softer and the voices went silent and little pinpoints of light appeared and pulsed and danced to the music and it was ecstatic and beatific, like being plugged in to God Himself. The little man played and played dancing his miraculous fingers up and down the keys. I sat there while the heavenly music played, eyes closed, and I'm sure people in the bar were looking at me but I didn't care, and I stayed like that after the Bach was done, floating back down to earth, and I didn't even clap for the poor man I was so entranced. Maybe he'd seen the look on my face and knew he had reached me and this satisfied him tremendously and I hoped that he had.

After he got his applause from a couple of others, the old man put the Bach back into his satchel and got more music out and played something lighter and more modern that I didn't recognize. I sat at my table and had a couple of more beers and finally the little man stopped playing and packed his music, rose for a final round of applause, took a little concert bow and left. I left soon afterward. As I was walking out the door, one of the billiard players gave a tremendous Navaho yell war whoop for some missed or made shot and rapidly apologized to the whole bar – "*sorry, sorry, sorry*" – and for one second I thought it was Win, that he had found me again, but it was only some Dutch model of Win, perhaps. I was so buzzed with all the beers by then that the yell did not startle me in the least as it did some of the others in the bar.

I walked and walked, past botanical gardens and into a pretty leafy treed part of the city. There was a zoo entrance and kids, little blonde round-faced Dutch doll kids and happy fathers and mothers and I marveled at how much joy and happiness could exist in this city. I sat and watched for a while from a bench but began feeling like a pedophiliac stalker and didn't want to alarm the parents or ruin the scene so I moved on. Great large bikes with tiny seats attached to the handlebars, bikes with slightly larger seats on the rear wheels, or even larger bikes with a wooden wheelbarrow box over the front served as minivans and transportation for these fathers and mothers. I would watch in amazement as two or three kids were piled in and the mother pedaled the whole contraption away with mighty thigh muscles.

I walked on down from the zoo and slipped into a museum dedicated to Holland during World War II. Entering, a series of drawings of stark wartime horrors and anti-Nazi propaganda lined the hall and then the stories of people, real people and their struggles and battles and failings and lives and deaths continued in the exhibit. There were heart-wrenching and hope-filling stories of people, some now dead, but some now grandmothers cooking delicious meals somewhere in this city. I walked through halls of remembered horrors and heroics, yellow stars ripped from dead unfortunates, the haunted eyes of those that later burned in ovens or were shot against some foul wall that I had earlier drunkenly puked on. Here truly were the wolves. I had walked into their emptied den, the foulness of their death stench still lingering in memories frozen in time.

I wandered into a small replica theater showing Nazi-era propaganda films and their happy-dumb-I'm-eating-your-children-behind-your-back music overlaying scenes of smiling strong youth doing acrobatics or pre-Fosbury Flop high jumps. I sat watching these idiot films for a while and thought of the crap I now watched on TV, and shuddered when similarities arose.

I got up and wandered into another room that had a detailed map of Amsterdam full of black dots, each dot representing a Jewish family. I stood and studied it all, retracing my steps of the previous days, looking at all these dots, each dot representing so much suffering and fear and horror, and I got closer and closer to the map until the dots filled my vision and there was one dot in front of me, tiny and looming in my mind. I thought of doors knocked down and smashing glass and cattle trains and hunger and ovens and I knew that very moment that if I were God I would smash a mighty fist down over the entire Earth and blot the whole of it out, sickened at my foul creation, and I was glad that I was not God but that someone better had the job.

I then came to a display that broke my heart. I'd seen it clichéd in movies a hundred times, the little girl that drops her doll as she is being carried off to unspeakable horrors, but here was the story for real and in front of me, something real that happened not too long ago and that doll fell on a street and spot that I had set foot on that day. I read the display softly, to myself, whispering the words under my breath and felt as if I were there watching.

"One day they rounded up Jews on a square in Amsterdam. I can still see a little girl pulling a wooden toy horse on a string. The cobblestones on the road made the horse fall over. The little girl wanted to put it back on its wheels, but a German soldier began to yell at her to keep walking. She was frightened and burst into tears. So did I."

And then I did too, not burst into tears but leaked one small tear onto the text of this exhibit. I wiped the tear away from the name of the person that had written the anecdote, someone named Jan Saumberg. I had to leave soon – the museum was just too much – but I feared going back out and walking around this city with war-opened eyes, feared that the beauty and joy I had seen would be gone and burned away and that I would only see horror everywhere. I thought of that little wizened man playing Bach in that bar while Nazi boots marched outside, and for a moment I was convinced that was exactly what he did, keeping some light and joy kindled in a long dark evil night, and this made me feel a little better.

I worked my way through the rest of the museum, knowing that we had won the war and surely there was a happy ending. Liberation Day had finally come and a long destructive five years had drawn to a close but it was not happiness but mostly numbness or recriminations or reconstructions that filled the void instead of joy or raucous celebration.

I wondered what Win would think of all this and if it would cure any of the Fox News-tinged racist conspiratorial attitudes he occasionally spouted like venom when he was sober, which was thankfully not often. I did not know. I thought it would wash over him probably, but maybe it wouldn't. In any case, it was time for me to leave. I had reached the end and it was time for me to go and face cold reality out there.

When I got out into that perfect sunny day, though, I immediately forgot the horrors of the past and enjoyed the bright beautiful warming summer afternoon, thankful to be living in the time between the frothy temporary madness that occasionally afflicts humanity. At least now the madness was in some far off shithole place in the world, not in a cool city like this. And that thought itself should have made me feel guilty and barbaric, but it didn't and I felt bad for not feeling guilty and for not being good, but I still enjoyed the day and walked on.

9
CASSIE

Over the course of my stay in Amsterdam I must have drunk gallons of Heinekens, Amstels, and to a lesser extent Duvels and La Chouffes, all in tiny increments in small glasses. This, coupled with the slow service, conspired to always keep me at the pleasant edge of drunk, but never quite over.

I walked from the Nazi museum seemingly forever, and felt the need to sit down and imbibe again. My recent two days of drug induced near solitude had left me with a need for human company. Female company, preferably. I felt good, ready, and hungry for it.

As I sat down in another outdoors bar on the Singel, a huge ruckus and laughter erupted from a table behind me and sitting at the epicenter of it all was Win. He saw me and yelled out, *"Dude!"* and motioned wildly for me to come over, grabbing a seat from the table beside him without asking. He was seated next to some hot blonde and three other people, one guy and two girls. He introduced me to Cassie, the hot blonde and the three others whose names I instantly forgot. I joined them and we sat and drank for a good long time and Win talked a hell of a lot. I mostly sat and listened, interjecting occasional witticisms that were lost on the three newcomers and on Win, though Cassie laughed at all of them. She was a laugh whore and I loved an easy audience; it made me talky. The group, college students from California, were on a whirlwind trip of the European capitals and seemed to be interested in my writing a guidebook, even one for Christians, and figured I would know a lot about the city. I explained that there was much more to this city than whorehouses and weed, such as unbelievable art, awesome architecture reflecting the golden age of the city, and on and on, but it seemed lost on them.

"Fuck that shit man," one of them, the guy, said. "I'm here to get stoned out of my gourd, dude. There's some bitchin' coffeeshops here and I've been to ten and I got twenty more to go." The two girls with him laughed and giggled. "As a matter of fact," he continued in an annoying surfer drawl, "fuck this place – let's go man!"

Win jumped up. "Let's do it man! Come on!" Win yelled to the world and grabbed the surfer guy by the shoulders and shook him and they took off and the two girls followed and everyone was carried along by the will and enthusiasm of the two. I got up with Cassie and we exchanged a look and walked behind them.

We walked for a bit and got to the large busy square of Leidseplein, which I had walked through approximately thirty-seven times on this trip alone. Win and Surfer Guy walked side-by-side, joking and punching each other and the two girls followed whispering between themselves and Cassie and I lagged behind. I joked a bit with her. She seemed to bring out my funny side with nice hearty sincere laughter at my lame, but occasionally hilarious, jokes and observations. She was a long leggy thing wearing short white shorts poorly chosen for the fickle climate here, but they did show off her sun-browned legs. She wore white canvas shoes and a simple white top – no guard against the temperamental elements. Her curly blonde hair was calculatedly disheveled. She was pretty, even beautiful, in a classic and effortless way without the need for makeup or pretense. I immediately liked her strongly and fell for her in the completely shallow but sincere way I often do with those girls I do not yet know. It's only when I start to know them that my interest wanes.

We all shot across Leidseplein and slipped into the Bulldog. The Bulldog is what a coffeeshop would be if they had coffeeshops in America, which is to say commercial and loud. It was a noisy familiar place and there were no Dutch there, not even working the place, only Eastern European wait staff and American tourists.

We went upstairs and sat surrounded by flashing lights and pop music and after a while we ordered drinks. I got a gin and tonic both because I was a bit tired of beer but also because I wanted to seem worldly and sophisticated to Cassie. Truth be told, it was actually a pretty decent gin and tonic, with honest tonic from a bottle not a soda gun and even a little plastic muddler for my lime.

Win brought out a pipe and some extremely good weed that he had bought elsewhere and we all smoked, myself included, and got extremely high. This stuff was strong and piney and heady, but being around Win made me want to at least try and keep up. Plus, I didn't want to seem like a prude in front of Cassie. She was smoking too and doing dumb and adorable things like trying to screw on the water bottle cap upside-down so it kept falling off and she did not understand what was happening and looked perplexed and we all laughed riotously at her.

It was a fun loud time but the strong weed soon made me edgy and paranoid. I imagined a multitude of plots going on in the bar, including an undercover agent using a *Pirates of the Caribbean* pinball machine he was playing to communicate secret coded messages by a series of beeps and bells to secret white slave traders lying in wait for delectable American morsels like Cassie here.

"This fine young specimen of California fresh and pure flesh here will bring in quite a princely sum to certain individuals in Saudi Arabia or Qatar, so let's get to dealing . . . how much for the blonde?" the slave trader would ask me and then I would be in a moral quandary – do I sell the girl I just met for a tidy good sum and buy a Maserati, or do I keep her for myself? Insane thoughts with only the barest tether to reality.

One shifty Palestinian did start talking to me as we all sat there, and I verified this later so I was not imagining it. He went on about how he was in the PLO and asked me lots of probing political questions and also told me how ninety-nine percent of the Senators and elected representatives of the United States are Jews and are responsible for all the ills of mankind. With me having recently come out of that Nazi museum, he'd caught me at the wrong time for that conversation. I wanted to break my gin and tonic glass on the guy's face, but I was mellow and pacific and told him simply and emphatically that he had his facts severely wrong. When he insisted that he knew, based on PLO sources, that he was absolutely right, I told him I was a Jew – which I'm not – and he looked squinty-eyed at me. Again I wanted to smash the heavy crystal ashtray over his skull and Win I think caught my murderous vibe and started loudly arguing with him and winning, since he was the loudest. I truly needed to leave right then and there, and I announced I was going to the park and asked if anyone wanted to come with me. Only Cassie expressed any interest and we both took off after I threw some Euros on the table and I told PLO once again that he was totally wrong and bid him *"Shalom."*

Cassie and I hurried out of that dark place into a shiny light-filled world outside and we both covered our eyes and then Cassie closed them and just stood there and basked in the sun, eyes closed, face to the sky, and her bronze skin was beautiful and perfect and she had a look of utter convincing contentment on her pretty face.

We walked a light stony walk through the square and laughed about the PLO guy and her water bottle and other things and wandered around in circles in Leidseplein for a while. The world seemed to wrap itself around me like an old movie where the screen moves amateurishly behind the character pretending to drive the car in the studio and things were floaty and not quite synced up with the motions of the occupants. We moved along airily in this fashion for a while, no one in the crowd bumping into us, and threaded our way past people coming at us from all cardinal points of the compass, avoiding wild trams, angry suicidal bicyclists and cocaine-fueled taxis.

I felt as if my body was leagues below me, a long marionette-stringed body being controlled expertly by some sentient entity above it all. I moved with ease and felt fantastic and in no time we had made it across a busy boulevard and into Vondelpark and we were on a broad tree-lined way before the park opened up in earnest to a huge forested expanse which swallowed the noise of the city.

We walked into the park without saying much. At some point we must have started holding hands because we were in fact holding hands. It was an effortless and natural thing and neither one of us thought much about it, I thought, and the ease of being with Cassie was wonderful and frightening at the same time. It felt like a dream, and a good one.

We sat on a sunny private spot with not too many people around us on the cool short intensely green grass and talked and even kissed a little and laid back on the grass looking up at the swiftly moving clouds, holding hands, me feeling the warmth of her body next to mine.

"That's an elephant wearing a hat," she said, staring up at the clouds.

"There's a dog eating a sausage," I said.

"That one is a tree with an apple falling from it," she said and giggled and we both lay there a while and did not say much, content.

We sat up and I told her of my amazing time in the national park and the hidden museum buried in the middle and the crazy trip home with Win's evil mushroom and the wild bike ride and she laughed and we kissed and her lips were soft as air and she smelled sweet like an expensive exotic candy. I stroked her golden curls and for a second we regarded each other. It was a very serious gaze, like we had exchanged some great never before spoken truth that only we knew and was precious and holy.

We both got up and went behind a stand of trees that was so shady you could not see the back and it was dark and cool in this private tree world. There was a hobo blanket wet on the ground but we did not lay there and instead found a pine needle bed and I put my coat down and we pressed our bodies together and there was almost palpable electricity between us lighting the dark copse of trees. Without a word we started kissing, sloughing off our clothes and making a tiny bed with them. We began making love and she rode me and her small firm breasts were food for me. The sun filtered through the trees and haloed her gold hair like she was the visitation of an angel.

When we were done we lay there quite a while saying nothing in particular, and she nestled in the crook of my arm and her head lay on my chest and I inhaled her sweet scent as her curly blonde hair tickled my nose, but it began to get cold and we put our clothes back on. I put my jacket on her California-issue outfit and she looked adorable and girlish in her short shorts, white top and substantial wool blazer, like she was wearing her dad's clothes. We held hands and walked in the park for a long time and had a beer at a large café in the middle of the park while blonde children played and tourists and locals alike shared the late August receding sun. All was truly right in the world at that moment, at least in my world.

"We really need to get you away from your travel buddies there," I said during our conversation. "I mean, you poor thing, you haven't even seen a Vermeer or Van Gogh, seen any of the history here, we gotta get you to go to one of the museums." I wanted to whisk her off and show her the world, travel with big steamer trunks and wear linen suits and dress her in flowered skirts, or throw on a backpack and see everything that was out there and never come home.

"I would love to see those paintings and see if I can see what you see," Cassie said in a smiling voice.

"It doesn't matter what I see, that only matters to me," I said. "What matters to you is what you see, what you get out of it, and it might be different or nothing at all or vice versa."

She smiled and we talked art for a bit and she had a surprising amount of knowledge on the subject, having taken and actually paid attention in an art appreciation class.

"Let's go then, let's go right now," I said. "Let's go to the Van Gogh Museum." It was still light and the museum would be open for a bit longer in the long summer day. I paid the bill and we left and strolled towards the Van Gogh Museum, which was right there nearby on Museumplein, walking through playing children that careened suicidally around the playground.

We waited and got in and basked underneath almond blossoms and starry night skies as only Van Gogh could paint them, as if he had unveiled a layer of reality to the magic miracle inner workings underneath everything and somehow made it available to those only willing to look. Cassie stood in front of one painting or another for long periods of time with wide-eyed, open-mouthed wonder and her eyes misted and I knew that she got it and that made her so much more attractive on a deeper and frightening level. Afterwards we sat in the museum café and had two café crèmes and talked about our favorites.

"I liked the portraits," she said, which was funny because I did not care for them much. "Just looking at the eyes he painted, like he spent half his time and paint on the eyes alone," she shook her head in amazement. "It was really cool."

We talked some more and it began to get dark and we were getting hungry. We walked out of the museum and back towards the canals. The night was cool and beautiful beyond belief and a half moon rose in the blue darkening sky and guided our way around the city.

We looked for a place to eat and saw a nice typically Dutch restaurant and got a small table all the way in the back where we could see the entire restaurant as it began to fill up. We sat and drank tiny cold beers. We talked and talked and ordered food and she got fish and chips and I got a tilapia in a lemon butter sauce and we ended up trading because mine was much better and I didn't mind. I wanted to give her the world at that point and felt heady like I was falling dangerously in love with her, and I was, and I hoped she felt at least a tiny bit the same.

"We're all going to Paris tomorrow," Cassie said during conversation and my heart sank. She caught my crestfallen expression and looked down at her plate sadly.

"You don't have to go you know," I told her, but I knew she would go.

"I know, but I gotta go, you know? They're like my friends and all," she said, and she was right.

"Maybe I can come with you," I said, ready to abandon my guidebook and Win. "I love Paris, I've been there like five times. I can show you around."

She smiled and touched my cheek in a surprisingly mature and tender gesture, and her touch lingered on there for a long time, even after she withdrew her hand.

"You've gotta finish your book," she said. "It's important." She looked at me with a mock stern look and added, "And besides, it's your job, mister."

I laughed. "Yeah, it is." She was unbelievably cute right then and I wanted to leap across the table and kiss her. "Maybe I'll catch up with you," I said, knowing that I wouldn't but it felt good to say anyway. I wanted to keep her, seal her away, kidnap her from her inane travel partners and hold her all for myself.

We finished our meal and lingered over dessert and two more café crèmes and the restaurant began to clear out and we sat there and talked and talked about art and travels and her friends and life back in San Diego and the amusing people in the restaurant that we made fun of in a light joking way. Finally, we were the next to last couple and I paid and we got up and walked out of the place.

We talked and walked the streets. The moonlight reflected off the inky black of the canals and the bridges were lit with tiny Christmas lights and it was ridiculously beautiful. It felt like we were walking in a postcard, but it was real and right in front of us. We stood on a bridge and looked out on the water shining with the moon above. I had my arm wrapped around her and I could feel the time slipping away between us and no matter how hard I hugged her it just kept slipping away.

It was getting late. It had to have been past midnight, and Cassie was leaving for Paris early as hell the next morning. We finally ended up at her hostel but none of her rowdy friends were there. She was staying in a dorm-type room and I wanted to be with her again but we couldn't do it in there and I knew better than to take her back to my primeval hotel room with Win hiding snakelike in the jungle bathroom. Even if he were not there, it would be impossible to explain, not to mention the fact that the room was disgusting.

We instead settled for sitting on the hostel steps in the cool night for what seemed like hours. We talked more and kissed and made out heavily in between the stragglers coming into the hostel from long party nights. We exchanged emails and numbers and promised to talk and I knew we would trade a few emails and maybe talk once or twice but that would be it and our lives would consume us once again and all that would remain would be a memory of one magic day in Amsterdam when love came down and kissed the earth. Even that memory would be swallowed by cruel time, I knew.

I was feeling sad as hell and we kissed goodnight, a long slow lingering angel kiss and she disappeared into the darkness of the door.

I walked through long lonely streets, with only streetlamps and canal ducks for company, the occasional lonely bike riding silently by, and dreaded the day ahead and made the night last as long as possible. I was finally exhausted and the day and night had caught up with me and if I didn't get sleep soon the wolves would be there feasting on my felled body. A lethargy borne of upcoming depression settled in on me and I cursed love for lifting me up to heaven briefly and then letting me drop into my mind's inky darkness. Without choice, I finally went to the hotel, was rung in after a while by the suspicious clerk and went up to the room, opening the door slowly and carefully. All was quiet and damp and I opened the window and Win was nowhere to be found. I collapsed into a bed stuck way in the corner, hugged my down pillow and went immediately to sleep without bothering to take my clothes off.

10
THE CALM

The wolves were hunting me down. I had slipped by unnoticed for a time but now I heard their baying calls and almost smelled their death dank cesspool breath upon me. I was running through a dark fairy-tale forest, branches low and ominous reaching down and scratching my face. Cassie was there running beside me, her arms and legs scratched by the branches, and she glanced at me with fear and confusion. A wolf howled and he was damn close, almost on me, and in a selfish fight-or-flight act of survival I pushed Cassie down and ran like hell. The forest got thicker and thicker and was dark, almost black now. A bush rustled with movement and the wolves howled and grunted from where I had left Cassie, and fear took hold of my throat. In the paralytic darkness I could feel one of them, their leader perhaps, pounce on top of me and put its ragged claw on my forehead and I tried to move but couldn't. I summoned an immense effort and with a great startle jumped awake and almost clean out of bed.

"Fuck man you scared the fuck outta me you fucking fuck!" Win yelled, jumping back from me.

In the fog-of-war morning my bleary eyes struggled to adjust and make sense of things. I at last realized that it was Win who was sitting beside me on the bed, probably messing with me, and that it had been Win's ragged fingernail on my forehead. Hadn't it? No telling. But my great awakening had startled the wolves away and made Win jumpy and I secretly smiled at myself for that.

"About time you fucking woke up. I was about to cut you open and see if you were still alive," Win said and scrambled up and started jumping up and down on the bed. "Let's go man I've got something I want to show you, and need a beer badly." The bed shook and I thought it would at least collapse, if not fall through the floor as well.

"Okay, okay," I said and rubbed my eyes, trying to triangulate, to pick up a signal and reestablish where I was, what had happened.

"What time is it?" I asked, rolling to my side and sitting up in bed. I leaned forward, resting my elbows on my knees, and put my head down, trying to will away the pounding headache.

"I don't know man but you slept through lunch and it's close to dinner," Win said.

I rummaged for a watch and found my green dialed square alarm clock. Six thirty, in the P.M., I assumed. Good heavens. How long had I slept for? Hours upon hours, though it felt like minutes. I rubbed my face again and padded to the bathroom.

"Give me a sec," I said to Win and he said, "Sure, sure," and milled about the room.

"Say, what's the deal with Monica here?" he asked, coming into the bathroom thumbing through the still crisp passport of Monica Wilma Schaffer which I had found among all the room's detritus days ago and had forgotten about.

"What do you mean?" I said as I washed my face.

"I mean where did this come from, this chick's passport?" he asked, with a disconcerting smirk.

"What do you mean, man? You must have picked it up from her, or did you have her over here the other night and did she leave it here?" I asked, looking at myself in the mirror. I looked like shit.

"I thought *you* had her over here the other night," Win said, and I could see him in a sideways reflection in the mirror, turning over the passport in his hands, but with a strange distant look in his eyes and I didn't think he could see me looking at him.

"Me? What the hell you talking about? I left you two in the coffeeshop," I said.

"Coffeeshop? You had to have had her over here because I didn't have her over here and she didn't just waltz in here and leave her passport here," Win said, still with a twisted half smile on his face, as if he were enjoying deliberately trying to mess with my mind.

"Stop messing with me. I know you had her over here. The room was a freaking mess. Either that or you lifted the passport from her," I said to Win, starting to grow annoyed.

"Fuck it man, you don't want to talk about it, that's cool," Win said and threw the passport over on the desk.

"You better find that poor girl," I told Win. "I'm sure she may want that passport to get back into her homeland and all. She's probably shitting bricks."

"Whatever," Win said dismissively. "You ready yet?" he asked impatiently.

"Let me shower real quick," I told him. I felt dirty as hell.

I closed the bathroom door and took small potted palm trees and broad-leafed tropical plants out of the shower and let the water run until it was nice and hot. I stripped and let it run over me and around me and through me. I soaked it up and slowly grew back to life and was suddenly hungry beyond belief.

I threw on some clothes and we left the hotel. It was colder now, but still pleasant. We walked down late afternoon streets, grey clouds threatening overhead, with Win jumping up and hitting the occasional elevated sign or post, jumping up quite high and making a huge noise when he slapped them with his big hands. "That's a basket!" he would say, or, "Three points!" and we walked along in this fashion until we got to a nice cozy restaurant I had been to before and we sat down and ordered an ungodly amount of food and Win picked at the large bowl of french fries.

"I thought you were hungry, man," I told him. "Look at all this food."

The table was covered with tiny well-charred and irresistible ribs and a large plate of pork satay in a delectable chocolaty peanut sauce and more fries and salad and bread and a large black iron cookpot of white wine scented mussels thrown in for good measure. I was ravenous and ate with lusty abandon, washing it all down with glass after glass of ice-cold Amstels. The food tasted fantastic and filled the emptiness in my belly beautifully.

I still felt off, even after the meal and after I ate most of the boozy chocolate mousse that Win ordered. My time with Cassie had thrown me off center, off myself and my own groove. It had been wonderful, but the sudden absence was now hard to take. I couldn't believe it had all been only one long day yesterday. I imagined her in Paris and pined for her and yearned to be there with her. It occurred to me that even if I went now, I would have no way of finding her except by luck or providence.

How many days and long nights had I been here anyway and how many days did I have left? I had no idea which day of the week it was even and how many lost days had washed unseen beneath me. I did know the hotel was keeping track and someplace in my spread out possessions, maybe, I had a printout with my return voyage home.

I pushed these thoughts away. There would be time enough for cold space capsule atmosphere reentry into so-called life later. Tonight, I was still in Amsterdam and I savored the feeling. I took another bite of delicious bread sopped in the white wine garlic mussel broth, which we had admonished the waitress to not take when she'd wanted to clear the table.

"So, man?" Win spoke up. He seldom talked while we ate. "How was she? You stole that little cutie from right under me. Man, oh man – I had plans for her, yes I did. I should go hunt her down and take her for myself is what I should do."

I grew suddenly incensed at the thought of Win's hands on Cassie.

"You stay the fuck away from her, okay?" I said a little more harshly than I meant to.

"Hey man, she's fair game, they're all fair game right?" Win said with a crooked half smile.

"Not her. She's off limits. You can have your hookers and your Monica, just leave Cassie out of it," I told him firmly.

"Man, she'd be a good one I think, I think the best, she was so hot and all so innocent looking, man oh man, I think she'd be the best one to do and I think that you think so too otherwise we wouldn't be having this discussion," Win said, still with that confident crooked smile on his face, like he knew something I didn't.

"We're not having this discussion. There is no discussion. She's off limits. *Verboten.* That's it. And besides, she's hopefully far away in Paris by now," I told Win, getting agitated.

"If you say so, man, she's in Paris. Sure. If you say so," Win said, still smiling. He was disconcerting me.

"She is and that's that. No Cassie, end of discussion," I said, and went back to sopping my bread in the white wine sauce.

We sat there quietly for some time, silently drinking beer after beer. I was slowly getting drunk. The thought of Cassie filled me with an empty desperation, as if she had grown roots inside me that were now ripped out. I needed to forget our day together and put her out of my mind. My dwelling on her would only cause me grief and ruin whatever was left of my trip.

I turned Win's vice-bloodhound nose to other pursuits to help me forget.

"Say, what's on for tonight? You got any ideas?" I asked him. I only wanted to go out and get wrecked and forgetful. To think about Cassie later when it wouldn't upset my voyage. I wanted to get wasted at least one last night with intent, and have a grand and debaucherous time here.

"Good good yes yes," Win said, perking up now and growing more animated. "I knew you'd come around. I got just the thing and I know and can see from your look that you got a little lovesickness there we gotta cure ASAP, you know?" Win said, picking up steam. "Some little cutie's messed with your noodle a little and we just gotta straighten out that noodle if you know what I mean, and I know that you know what I mean," Win went on in his rapid fire too loud voice, a red vein pulsing on his forehead like he would explode with words if he didn't get them out fast enough.

"First things first what we gotta do is get outta here. So here's what we do, we walk out, you pay the bill and we'll get right now to the nearest coffeeshop and get you something nice and strong to wipe the memory. Start from a clean slate and all that. We'll go on from there to something else that I've got in mind and have had in mind and have been planning for a long time since we got here. Cool?" Win shot out at me.

"Planned? What do you have planned?" I asked, suspicious now.

"Don't you worry, it's something you wanted, don't worry." He grinned.

I rubbed my temple, feeling the headache coming back, but shook it off.

"Let's go," I said, resigned to my fate now that I'd put Win's wheels in motion. I was doomed the moment I had put myself into his hands, but between being a victim and a volunteer, I foolishly thought that being a volunteer would be better. I got up, paid, and went out into the cold damp night, the air now pregnant and anticipatory with rain.

11
THE GARDEN OF EARTHLY DELIGHTS

We walked down the road and over one canal to Spui, an area of restaurants and a couple of nice coffeeshops. We ducked into one of the coffeeshops just as it started to rain and grabbed a table. Win left for the bar and came back quite a bit later juggling coffees and several tiny bags and threw all the bags down on the table before setting down the coffees. The small translucent wax paper bags of drugs rained down on me. Win set the coffees down nearly spilling them, the small saucers awkward in his big hands.

"Good fuck this place is small, I'm taking up half the place," Win said.

It *was* small, a tiny postage stamp of a place, all oriental rugs and red painted walls and heavy dark stained wood furniture. It was pleasingly cozy and opium den womblike. Its stoned denizens sat on tiny stools or stood dripping wet from the rain outside – it was really raining buckets. We relaxed, settling in at our prized table, glad that we got here when we did. Win fiddled with a pipe and handed it and a lighter to me.

"You first, buddy," Win said, smiling.

I took them and lit the pipe, a small golden nugget of hash lit up, sweet smelling and with smooth mellow smoke that I hit three more times before emptying out. I grew tendrils out of my ass and my legs rooted firmly to the ground, and they felt wooden. I merged into my stool and anyone could have come sat on me at that moment but thankfully they didn't. The smoke in the tiny place formed a thermocline with my head completely in it. Win gave a devilish smile and sucked on the pipe like a diver dying for oxygen.

I sat there for quite a while and breathed twice in fifteen minutes, so it felt, and I stretched my neck and circled my head and time slowed to a crawl and for a frightening moment I thought it had stopped altogether and I was terrified that it would not start back up. It did, and I breathed easier, though all was still turtle slow.

People came and went from the tiny place and we sat there and smoked. I had barely touched my coffee and Win leaned back and spread out as best he could on the minuscule chair, looking around with slitted eyes.

"You should play chess with that guy, man," Win said, backhanding my arm and pointing with his finger in one smooth move. I turned and looked where he was pointing and it took a few seconds for the image to settle back into itself. When it did, there was a man at the other end of coffeeshop playing chess with some hapless tourist. The man looked dapper and well dressed in a vintage suit and had slicked-back black hair and a pencil moustache and pointed goatee and a mischievous and evil glint in his coal eyes. He looked like a villain from a 1930's cliffhanger.

"What, that guy there?" I asked in a slow molasses voice.

"Yeah," Win nodded slant eyed and grinned, "it would be a match for the ages."

The slick man was playing, and winning, a chess game, his smooth black pieces outnumbering his ill-fated ivory opponent by a large margin. Black bishop to white queen and now the tourist was screwed completely.

"No way dude," I said, a wave of dread and foreboding washing over me. "That's the devil himself there. There's no winning your soul back from that." I shook my head. "Checkmate, dude."

Win gave a scheming grin. The man did look like a villain from a silent film, and I envisioned some beautiful heroine tied to a tram track somewhere in the city, waiting for him to come back and cackle maniacally and twirl his mustache while she struggled all innocent and wide-eyed. The dapper man won the chess match and he started rearranging the pieces. He caught me staring and looked intently at me as if inviting me and challenging me. Suddenly and horribly, his face changed from being a caricature to hardening and taking on a malevolent and frightening countenance. For one startling moment I truly believed that the man was actually the Devil. The devil man smiled at me and a torrent of menace hit me like a fist and wolves howled in the distance and my head swam and I closed my eyes because I could not stand his gaze. I opened my eyes again and he still stared at me and my head still swam and now drowned and I couldn't move. But then the devil man stopped looking at me. My eyes regained their focus and I came back to myself again.

"We have got to get the fuck out of here right the fuck now, man," I told Win slowly and deliberately, and added, "His minions are coming." Win gave me a sideways glance without moving his big head, but didn't say anything, merely accepted my insane announcement as true.

"I hear you, man," Win said. "Let's hit this again and we go," and Win handed me the hash pipe and we smoked it hurriedly, but the threat subsided and that vacuous opium den vibe returned to the place. I looked up at the devil man, steeling myself for his repellent look, and the guy was gone. Just like that. He had slipped out and I hadn't seen him.

"Win, did you see that devil leave?" I asked Win very seriously.

"No dude," Win said behind half closed stony eyes.

"You didn't see that?" I asked, agitated. "The fucker just vanished in a wisp of smoke in front of us. He's got our number for sure now."

"Man, a fuckload pack of wild apes wearing tutus could have can-canned past here and you wouldn't have noticed, you're so stoned," Win said matter-of-factly without a trace of emotion.

"No, no," I shook my head, "he vanished, dude, he vanished just to let us know the score of the game." I was convinced, though Win was probably right.

"Let's get outta here, it's time," Win said, slowly lifting off the seat, rising like an apparition.

I rose as well, peeling my roots from the ground with a great effort, and stumbled over one of the tiny tables almost knocking over the drinks of some square-headed German tourist who glared at me maliciously but did not say anything. I wobbled and caught my balance and we spilled out onto the street.

Then something happened, one of those things that defy belief. One of those stories someone tells you and you nod and smile but disbelieve nonetheless. Win, walking a couple of steps ahead of me, stepped off of the curb into the bike path. A bicycle whizzed by, seeming to go through Win, to actually go through him as if he were a ghost.

"Did you see that, man?" I said excitedly. "That bike went through you. What the hell? Did you feel that?"

"Whoa," was all Win said, stepping back onto the curb. "That was weird."

No explanation was forthcoming or even possible and when something like that happens you start doubting it even if it happened just a very short while ago. It was easier to blame it on the drugs, so I did.

Convinced we were under some cosmic or divine protection, we tore ahead recklessly through the streets, Win taking chances with the traffic and the bicycles, convinced of his immortality at this point. Win walked fast, leading me to who knows what, and I felt like a balloon on a tether floating serenely above the cool summer night streets of Amsterdam. Thoughts and revelations fluttered in and out of my mind like sparrows attacking breadcrumbs. I was not able to peg anything down, though I felt like I was on the edge of some great discovery. At that moment, nothing was in the future and nothing was in the past and, for a very brief moment, there was no "I," only a poor completely lost soul floating through ghost streets and it was wonderful and horrifying all at the same time. With a great effort of will, I winched myself down from my highwire and slipped back into myself. It was comfortable, like slipping into a pair of well-worn jeans after trying on clothes at a store all day.

Win navigated the streets like a pro, walking and never breaking stride. Bicycles and trams and cars and people seemed to flow around him. I tried to keep up but my rhythm and pulse were off and I kept running into people and got honked at by a couple of cars and I lost count of how many bicyclists' grimacing faces I saw from entirely too close. Win walked relentlessly like a man on a mission to whatever big surprise he had in store for me.

We ducked into a seedy looking bar.

"This it?" I asked.

"Not yet, more drink first," he said.

We knocked back a couple of quick beers and moved on, spilling coins on the bar and not even waiting for a bill or change. We repeated this at another bar that looked like a prostitute hangout, leaving Euro Monopoly money this time and a waiter nicely chased us down to give us the change but we told him to keep it and judging from his surprised and happy face it was a very large tip indeed.

The streets turned old and seedy and we were seventeenth-century sailors off the ship on shore leave, ready for rowdy times and women. Win got into a scuffle with some Americans near the Bulldog – the other Bulldog in the Red Light District, not the Leidseplein one – but they were too stoned and in no mood or shape for fighting, only monkey-shit-throwing words of bravado. We walked on past the *Sex! Sex! Sex!* shops in every variety and permutation: straight, gay, women, BDSM, gay BDSM, gay women, gay BDSM women, and so on. Scratch deep enough and you could find anything in this place, which is what I was beginning to be afraid of.

"We're going in here," Win said suddenly at a pastiche theater front touting *Sexy Sex Show Live Sex!* Red peeling paint and burned-out bulbs ringing a marquee decorated the place and Win talked to a guy sitting in a tiny ticket booth for a very long time and I stood there, head swimmy and disconnected from my body. After a while the transaction seemed finished and some dubious Arab appeared from a side door and led us away from the place, which it turned out was only an empty façade, to the sex show proper. Win lit a huge cone joint and smoked half of it in three drags before handing it to me and I dragged on its minty pine goodness and it was heady and mind expanding pot, really top notch gear, and it neatly trimmed off the remainder of the roots I had and really went to my head.

We followed this short Arab through half the Red Light, back past the Bulldog and the Americans sitting at outdoor tables who didn't notice us. We turned down strange side streets lined with red-lit meat lockers of every imaginable flesh: short fat Filipinos and tall Dutch blondes and tiny bored Mexican women and dark-haired menacing Croatians. I began to feel their desperate eyes on me. The pot was making me self-contemplative and empathic and also paranoid and this fucking Arab leading us to who knows where and what was getting to me. I told Win as much.

"Win," I whispered in his ear, holding on to his arm for balance, "this fucking guy is getting to me. Where is this murderous Arab taking us?"

"Chill out man, it's okay," Win said, shaking free of my hold on him.

"Nah, he's gonna slit our throats in some dank alley. Our blood will run into the canals," I insisted.

"You're just being paranoid, man," he said, hitting me on the arm. "Chill out."

I walked on nervously. At last, we arrived at some once beautiful but now worn out and spoiled canal house. The Arab guy went up to a nondescript door and knocked and some other shifty Arab opened it and Arab #1 handed us off to the guy inside who swung his arm wildly beckoning us in with an insincere smile ripped into his face, like we were at a bazaar buying rugs.

"I'm not going in there," I said, shaking my head and crossing my arms. "What are you getting us into, what the fuck is in there?"

"Come on dude, it'll be great," Win said, flashing his huge charismatic-as-hell smile. "It's a good show, man, I've been working on this for days since we got here, I already paid for it, it'll be great come on!"

Win walked in.

I stood outside for what seemed like an eternity, my mind trying to piece together fragments of disjointed facts and images. A deep-seated feeling that there was something very wrong and unspeakable there began to take hold of me, something that I was somehow responsible for. Arab #1 stood glaring at me now, not with an insincere smile but with a threatening scowl and my mind swam in dark canal waters and wolves howled from distant woods and without any seeming choice I entered the black maw of that house and darkness swallowed me.

We walked down a narrow hallway lit with tiny dim red sconces going from patch of faint red light to patch of faint red light past chasms of darkness, stepping on threadbare once lovely but now horror-movie-tattered rugs that slithered under our feet. We came to a door and shifty Arab #2 knocked and some huge Nordic blonde guy with a square Frankenstein head, minus the bolts, opened the door and invited us in. We went up rickety stairs and now everything was movie-like and I thought and was convinced we would walk into some red meat horror torture chamber but we didn't and walked into a large room with a bar and bar stools arranged around a central slightly raised stage. A few decrepit people sat around on stools at the edges, sheltered in the darkness. We finally sat down, waiting there for God knows what to start.

"What the fuck is this, dude?" I asked Win.

"You'll see man," Win said, all mysterious. "It'll make you feel better, it'll be great. It's what you wanted, you'll see."

We sat there on small stools and waited. The weed was still in full effect; it had hit me hard, and now I was thirsty and parched as hell.

"The fuck is there to drink around here?" I asked to no one.

As if she'd heard, a tired dead blonde appeared behind us and took our drink order and had us pay a hell of a lot up front and she returned with two very tiny – tinier than usual, even – beers. I drained them and it was a mistake because she did not come back for a very long time, and also because I dreaded going to the bathroom in a place like this. I knew there would be a squad of gay bears in the bathroom ready to jump me and do unspeakable things to me and render me a eunuch for life, so I resolved to hold it in no matter what and pee myself if I had to.

The lights went down and my heart started thumping and I had no idea what was going to come out on that stage. Somehow, I suspected that nice clean-cut blonde strippers were not on the agenda. A tiny door opened towards the back of the stage and two small midgets came out carrying a table, which they placed carefully in the middle of the stage. One of them waddled back and brought out a rickety wooden chair too. They both disappeared back through the door.

A spotlight shone on the table and empty chair and another bigger door opened and a muscular and not unattractive woman came out in a tiny bodybuilder bikini. She walked around the stage by the bar, eyeing the patrons sitting there, ourselves included, and took off her top revealing two hard muscular breasts. There was no music or anything, only the empty hollow sounds of her padding barefoot on the wooden floor. She sat down on the chair and spread her legs and undid a string and her bikini bottom fell away.

The muscle woman then gave an amazing and disgusting show, feats of vaginal strength that I scarcely thought possible involving a variety of objects from the table including bowling pins, staplers, bananas and so on. It was very sideshow-freaky and Win laughed uproariously every time the muscle lady switched to a new prop, punching me on the arm, which now had a bluish honest bruise welling from inside.

The show was like a car wreck and I couldn't turn away. The act culminated in a piercing straight through her labia with a large needle and a basket of tulips that swung from a string threaded to it between her legs. She did not wince and took the pain like some freak yogi and again I could not turn away. The spotlight went dark and she undid her predicament and walked back to the door and out and a couple of people gave halfhearted claps and I didn't know whether to clap or not or what to do so I sat there stunned and did nothing. The two midgets came out into the darkness and took away the chair and table and tainted props.

"What the fuck was all that?" I asked. The slurred and stoned question dripped out of my mouth. Win did not answer but giggled crazily instead.

The lights around us impossibly dimmed more and little red Christmas lights turned on that ringed the bottom and top of the stage and another strange door opened in the wall. Round two of the entertainment came out.

She was tall and lithe, though a little skeletal, and had a tired weary face that had probably once been pretty and even stunning in a dark-haired Eastern European way, but now looked spent. She wore standard old-school stripper clothes, with little tassels on her cone bra, even. Slowly, these came off in stages as she danced and prowled around the stage, again with no music. Soon she was completely nude. She had small tits and a very hairy pussy that Win pounded me on the arm and commented on, giggling maniacally in my ear.

The stripper then prowled around the stage to one end of the bar and fixated on one poor fucker sitting opposite us, some lonely bespectacled caricature of a dirty old man, the archetype from which all dirty old men caricatures spring.

"You want sexy fuck?" the stripper asked in a Russian or Eastern European accent, the words dripping from her mouth, a bored and tired proposition that no one took her up on. She made her way around the bar and eventually to us and repeated the question. I couldn't look her in the eye or look away either, so I looked at her pale forehead, and it looked like the sun had not touched her in six hundred years. The only thing that gave her a human complexion was the glow of all the red lights around her.

She went up to Win and wearily asked the same question. Win winked and smiled at her and then laughed and for a second I thought he was going to have himself a sexy fuck, but he didn't. He was only messing with her and the look of utter disdain on the stripper's face could have cut down a buffalo or ripped all humanity from whoever crossed her razor-wire gaze.

The stripper finally gave up on her solicitation and went to the middle of the room, grabbed a humongous dildo the size of my arm that had been placed there by an unseen midget, and proceeded to fuck her gaping alien-mouthed pussy right there in front of us. It was like a bloody highway fatality accident, and I felt inhuman watching it but could not turn away. Win laughed and punched me in the arm. The fucker kept hitting me in the same spot. He shouted obscenities at the stripper, stating the obvious – "Oh man, look at that bitch's pussy, open wide!" and so forth.

I began to tune out Win and the stripper as best as I could and retreat into myself, to find my happy place. When I looked at her, I could not see even a trace of humanity in her dried husk exterior, and that scared the hell out of me more than anything else. I should have at least felt sympathy or horror or revulsion or outrage but I felt nothing at all at that moment, only utter absence. I sat there with a glazed look and some vague far-away feeling that I had been anesthetized and that the wolves were silently feasting on my raw meat leg already. I shook off these terrible thoughts and began to feel hot, which at least was a feeling, and I desperately wanted to leave.

Finally, the stripper stopped working her dildo, flashed one last disdainful castrating look at everyone in the bar, and exited through that tiny crazy door into whatever hooker underground vault she lived in or was kept in. I sat there, the weed still going strong in my head but beginning its final descent into normality – or what passed for it here. I stared at the empty stage for a long time, empty minded, and the skeletal stripper mercifully receded into repressed nightmare memories.

I sat and stared at the little red lights, tiny night landing strips of some forlorn hell airport flytrap waiting for fool victims. The little red lights blurred and my eyes watered and I stared and did not close my eyes for a very long time and the red lights grew slightly to distinct tiny red pentagrams lining the room all in a row. At this sight, my heart raced and I felt sudden panic hit me like a fist. I had to warn Win but the words that came out of my lips were gibberish.

"Red witchcraft here," I warned Win, who sat looking around expectantly. "Danger and peril. Beers elsewhere. Next hooker will have our heads," I raved like a frothy-mouthed madman.

"Chill out dude. She'll come out soon. She'll come out," Win said and turned and looked at me, smiling reassuringly, but his head was grotesque and his smile was a jagged scar carved into a meat pumpkin. I tried to breathe deeply and maintain, hoping and praying it was the drugs or booze or exhaustion twisting my reality and not unending madness setting in.

Panic started creeping up my back and it was getting very hot in there. The *Caligula*-like weirdness of the previous acts had me on edge. Suddenly I heard, clear and distinct, wolves howling, close, and almost jumped off my stool. A small tight spotlight flicked on from somewhere and shone in the center of the stage and the lights around us went dark and blackness crept in from behind. The red pentagram lights turned off, leaving faint ghosts where they had been. Everything was quiet and all I could hear was my heavy breathing and my pulse pounding in my head.

A small man came out of the darkness and into the center spotlight and – *holy good fuck!* – it was the devil man from the chess game at the coffeeshop! My head swam and reeled, not knowing what to make of this. I hopelessly wished that I was imagining him, but he seemed very much real and in front of me.

"Ladies and gentlemen," he said in a smooth and seductive voice, even though there were no ladies in the audience, or gentlemen either if you wanted to get technical about it, "you have paid to see a show, the show of all shows, full of all that is life and all that is death. You have wanted more and more, ever more." He turned, paused and looked straight at me. "And now you shall have it," he continued. "I warn you, this 'more' you want is quite powerful and strong, quite more than you can handle, as you wanted, so those with weak stomachs please leave now."

The few guys that were in the room slowly, one by one, left through the sheltering darkness; I could hear their scuffling feet on the dusty creaky wooden floor. I wanted to leave too, to follow them somehow back into the cool night outside and went to get up but Win held my shoulders down. I looked up at him and he was huge, a horror nightmare vision of a wolf breathing fetid air on me. I froze in panic and gasped for air in the hot and unbearably stuffy room.

The devil man gave an enormous too-big-for-his-face Cheshire Cat smile and receded into the darkness. As I waited in the pregnant darkness, terror setting in, I wanted to leave more than ever. I tried again but Win's clawed hands pressed down on me. The spotlight shut off with a loud click and ice water poured down my spine. The room was completely astonishingly dark and silent and I never would have thought that darkness and silence could be so horrific.

A huge switch was thrown somewhere with a loud clunk and another spotlight appeared in the other side of the room. I jumped. Huge booted footsteps echoed through the darkness for what felt like eternity and into the light emerged some stitched together monstrosity, not quite human, dragging a rope. It stepped into the light long enough to inspire fear and horror, and then it disappeared into comfortable darkness at the side of the stage. At the end of the rope on tied hands was beautiful tanned maiden skin and – good fucking shit! — *it was Cassie*!

The blood drained from my veins, spilling onto the filthy semen-stained floor.

Cassie stood in the middle of the spotlight with her gaze darting fearfully around into the darkness, like a cornered rabbit, eyes wide with terror. Her beautiful innocent face was smudged with dirt and she was barefoot and her white clothes were dirty. Her top was ripped and barely hanging on her and she tried to cover herself but her hands were tied and pinioned, held to the beast in front of her that she was desperately trying to stay away from. I wanted to call out to her but nothing came out of my mouth and it occurred to me that she could probably not see me hiding in the darkness and she was alone with that horror out there. There was a pregnant silence in the air and in between my own breaths and Win's ragged putrid breaths I could hear Cassie breathing hard and fast, almost hyperventilating.

More footsteps manifested now in the darkness. Cassie's head swung around and her eyes went even wider. I wanted to look away and tried but couldn't. Win held my head up with one furry rough beast hand, forcing me to watch as a procession of abominable creatures and people lined up to ravage and despoil Cassie. One by one they came, and Cassie fought in vain against them with tied hands. I wanted to jump up and rip them apart and rain holy fire and death upon them, but Win held me tight, like a wolf biting down on my neck savoring his prey. His fetid carrion breath wafted over me and I screamed but nothing came out and I couldn't turn away.

Horror after horror came at Cassie and she struggled as best she could at first but she soon lost strength as she was violated horribly again and again. I wept as her humanity was taken from her before my eyes, and started losing strength myself. I tried punching at Win but my arms did not cooperate, as if they were not my own. Win stood behind me, gripping me tighter and tighter and now nothing but rabid animal grunts and insane wolf laughter came from him. I could barely breathe and didn't want to, hoping I would die or pass out by holding my breath but my body betrayed me and took in the vile air around me.

An interminable hellish time later, a barely recognizable Cassie lay in a defeated bruised heap on the floor, her soulless eyes staring out into nothingness. The devil man came out to Cassie under the spotlight, and I was convinced now it was the Devil himself and that this was Hell, that it had been here on Earth the whole time and not underground in flaming caverns.

"Let us give a big round of applause for our entertainment this evening," the Devil said and unseen fiend hands clapped their approval. Beside me, Win, or whatever it was, gave a guttural inhuman grunt.

"And now for the big finale," the Devil said and reached over to Cassie's beaten used body. He grabbed her by her sweat-matted hair, lifting her up with inhuman strength and brought out a knife. Slowly, he carved across her throat, and blood sprayed out like something from a movie. A horrible death gurgle bubbled out of her and her beautiful green eyes went wide with surprise and shock then went horribly far away, dead. I tried to scream again and this time I did scream, loudly and endlessly and wolves howled in approval and Win snarled and growled expelling poison air and somewhere underneath the howling madness in the faraway night outside, a church bell tolled three long strokes. And then I knew only darkness.

12
ONE LOVE

Gentle mother hands shook my shoulders, rocking me tenderly awake from whatever dark dreamworld I had been living in. I blinked and bright sun haloed a kind grandmother visage, white curly wispy hair ringing a wrinkled and soft face. "Yaya," I called out from some dreamworld far below the depths. I blinked.

". . . take care of you," the grandmother angel called out from a sunny light filled world.

"I know you will, Yaya," I called out from fathoms deep.

". . . must leave," the gentle grandmother said, leaning over and shaking my shoulders. I opened and closed my eyes and tried to move my head.

"You must leave now. I will call police to take care of you," the grandmother said again in her Dutch accent, giving me another shake.

At the word "police" my eyes snapped open and neurons fired and synapses closed and the dark red blood horrors of last night flooded back and filled the sky with gloom. My heart raced and a throbbing vein pulsed in my head. I leaned up onto my elbows and looked around. A fine canal house loomed above me as I lay in a tiny well-manicured garden with a black clad stern-faced and scared grandmother standing there, hands on hips. I rose too fast and my head swam and alien buzzing insects sang a chorus inside my skull. The grandmother stepped back, startled and frightened at my sudden move.

"Thank you, sorry, sorry," I muttered to her from a hollow raspy dry throat and my voice sounded strange and harsh and not at all my own, like I had been screaming or grunting all night.

I stumbled away, walking in any direction, wanting to put some distance between myself and this poor old woman who had woken up on this fine damp morning to find some drunk stoned loser lunatic bedding down for the night in her lovingly cared-for garden, leaving crushed hydrangeas and begonias in his foul wake.

I walked in a daze for a few yards and had to stop. The ringing in my ears grew all encompassing and my vision blurred. My leg started twitching then jackhammering on the ground. I broke into a cold sweat of fear. *So this is what dying of a stroke feels like*, I thought to myself, but I did not die. The feeling washed over me like a murderous wave, leaving me reeling and gasping for air in its cold skeleton-depths undertow. I held onto a tree for a moment while the grandmother eyed me warily from three doors down. I made an effort to walk again and ducked into the first small side street I came to and disappeared from the poor grandmother's view forever, I hoped.

The tiny alley spat me out onto another canaled avenue and I looked around to get my bearings and saw that I was at the edge of the Red Light District again, and then flashes and visions of the night before hit me like a crowbar to the face. *Cassie.* Good fuck what had happened? Had I really seen all that? Where was Win? *What* was Win? Good fuck, what was going on? My head swam again and that alien buzzing returned, getting even louder.

I saw a bench and stumbled towards it and poured myself into it and sat glazed-eyed. The early morning-after hangover day marched relentlessly on in front of me. Sanitation workers drove tiny spinning brushed vehicles up and down the streets, sucking up the detritus of the previous night. I eyed them cautiously, hoping I wouldn't get sucked up with all the filth. The noise as they drove by was unbearable and made me want to scream but my throat was raw and would have none of it. I rubbed my eyes and my fingers felt wet and when I looked at them they were pinkish red with a thin film of blood. In my morning fog stupor, I stupidly tasted the blood, licking it off my fingers. My head reeled again and now my stomach gave a warning flip. I bent over and wiped my hands clean on my shirt. There was not that much blood, only a little, and it blended into the black fabric. I hoped it was my own, from some new wound or maybe from where I had hit my head against the sink, and not someone else's. Not Cassie's.

I sat, my mind reeling and trying to work through the fog and the buzzing. Already, the previous night seemed more and more like a hallucination. It couldn't have been real. I didn't want it to be real. The only way to know for sure was to find Win.

The bench imparted its stability to me and in a short time I felt able to walk. I had no immediate plan but to get back to the hotel and find Win. I also desperately wanted to shower in hot boiling water, take off my tomato skin befouled exterior and see if there was anything good and clean left underneath it. I looked in my wallet, which to my surprise I still had. I had twenty Euros and a smattering of change. I considered taking a cab but rethought it given my no doubt alarming appearance and scant funds.

I rose from the bench and wound my long way back to the hotel. I vacillated between analyzing what had happened and trying to push it away to a deep dark place of forgetting, to some fetid oubliette of darkest depth that it could fall into and never be seen or heard from again. Already the events of the previous night seemed unreal, like a Hieronymus Bosch surreal hellscape. Had I really seen Cassie get raped and murdered? Was it all some mind-bending hallucination given to me by Win in a gross abuse of Shamanistic powers? Was Win really a shape shifting werewolf inhuman fiend demon? It could not be. I had to find Win. Even he had some shred of humanity, surely, and last night's ritual sacrifice, if that was indeed what it had been, could not have gone unnoticed by him.

I walked on, but my head swam again and insects buzzed. I leaned against a wall and closed my eyes and I heard Nazi screams and the echo of gunfire from seventy years ago and saw, in my mind, a bullet with brain and skull go through me and carve a small crater into the wall. Old ghosts wailed and hungered for justice. I shook my head and moved on, convinced I was going insane now, and this was actually comforting because it explained a lot.

I walked out of the Red Light District and down that same windy alley of millennia ago and, of course, the Rastafarian gypsy was walking towards me with his guitar, only he had it out now and was playing. The music filled the alley and it was quite beautiful. The gypsy was playing Bob Marley, singing:

Is there a place for the hopeless sinner
Who has hurt all mankind just to save his own?
Believe me,
One Love, One Heart
Let's get together and feel all right
One Love, One Heart
Give thanks and praise to the Lord and I will feel all right.

He walked towards me singing this and smiling and I stood there and the music filled me and fed me and I felt about a million times better. I got out my twenty Euros and tried to give it to him even though he was not asking for anything, only playing out of the abundance of his heart. I smiled at him and a short happy laugh escaped from me. It was a small strange and insane cackle. The gypsy walked on though, paying me no mind, playing his guitar and singing. The music followed him down the alley and I could hear him for a long time after as I stood alone in the middle, the wind blowing papers and garbage around me. He went on singing: "*There ain't no hiding place from the Father of creation, sayin' One Love, One Heart, let's get together and feel all right . . .*"

When the background noise of traffic and the city finally drowned out the gypsy's music, I started my walk again. As soon as the music left the heaviness and darkness returned and I shook my head to try and clear the buzzing.

I walked out of the alley, crossed the street by the Krasnapolski Hotel, and was at Dam again, at the morning shadow of the huge stone obelisk looming in front of me. I crossed the empty square and went up its steps and got close to the obelisk. I was unable to negotiate the steps, though, and stumbled and fell and hit my knee hard and winced and got back up. Now my head was really buzzing with infernal insect noises and when I closed my eyes all I could see were Cassie's beautiful green eyes wide with surprise and fear and slowly being drained of life. Panic and despair welled up inside me.

I needed to sit down or fall down, and I made my way to the front of the obelisk. I collapsed and began to cry, slowly at first. Then, inexorably, I wept and wept, a flood I could not stop. I felt empty and I was a parched desert with a giant dam built all around me, holding nothing and everything back. Something in my throat scratched and clawed at me, like something horrible had crept in and was trying to crawl out. The world spun and I looked up and there, looming above me, was Christ floating on the obelisk. At that moment, I prayed, actually really and sincerely prayed. *I'm sorry, please let it all have been a dream, let Cassie be alright,* I prayed, and repeated it over and over, but nothing happened, Superman did not spin the world backwards.

I closed my eyes trying to hold back the tears inside but I wept and the tears now seemed like they were flowing inside me. They watered my desert and I felt water rising inside and the creature in my throat thrashed as the waters rose. I let out one unearthly sound from within that petrified me and then the dam burst and I felt water gushing out of me and the creature, all indescribable insect darkness and horror, escaped into the clear day and howled in pain at the light and vanished. I knelt on the hard stone and wept and all I could say was "Oh God," repeating it over and over, until a searing but cool light filled me and I passed out.

The stone was cold and pleasant beneath me, and for a moment I knew that I was dead and lying in marble in some tomb. Somewhere, a carillon's bells rang from a bell tower and it was Bach, gloriously ringing in the new day. I looked up and there was light everywhere and the obelisk loomed above me and Christ still hung there gazing patiently at me. The bells finished their song and rang eight, and when they stopped I realized that I was alive, gloriously alive, and lying in the middle of the Dam. I rolled to the side and sat up, taking one deep breath. My throat felt fine and normal now and my head slowly cleared. I rose and was a bit unsteady. I felt light and empty, but in a pleasant unencumbered way, and I took a few tentative steps down from the monument, turning around and taking one more look at the huge obelisk and the open arms of Christ stretched out there.

I walked on, feeling better but pretty far from normal. As I walked I felt lighter and better, and soon I was almost running through the streets towards the hotel, anxious to talk to Win, to see and confirm what the hell had happened in that club. The thought did occur to me that if he was, in fact, a wolf monster in league with the Devil, I had no backup plan. But I had to find out.

I raced through the Spui to our hotel and darted through the lobby past the clerk who was busy with a gaggle of pink cowboy hat wearing women there for a hen party. Bounding up the stairs to our floor, I went past the elevator and walked on down the hall towards Room 315. I slowed, and came to the door. I stood there and took a deep breath.

Cautiously, I opened the door to our room. At first I thought I was in the wrong room and swung around and looked at the outside of the door, 315, and it was right. The room had been re-arranged to how it looked at the beginning, with everything in its place and clean. Win was nowhere to be seen and, indeed, there was no evidence that he had ever even been there. My head swam a little, though with nowhere near the undulations it had given before, more like an echo of the past.

I stumbled into the bathroom and it was immaculately clean. The botanical tropical garden was gone, except for a beautiful little orchid with gorgeous tiny blood red flowers that sat on the vanity, doubled against the mirror. Leaning against the orchid was a note, written in Win's lunatic scrawl, reading simply:

> I'M GONE.
> FOR NOW.
> YOU SHOULD BE 2.

I picked up the note written on the fine linen stationary of the hotel. Behind it, leaning against the orchid, was a passport. I picked it up. Darwin J. Jones, it read. Odd. He'd left his passport here.

I took the passport and thumbed through the pages filled with stamps. Berlin, Germany. Madrid, Spain. Paris, France. Amsterdam, Netherlands. I thumbed to the back to his picture and the blood drained from my face.

There, smiling back at me, was my own face. Shaved, hair shorter and neatly combed, and unmistakably me.

I leaned on the vanity, looking down at the picture, and cold fear spread over me. I wanted to look up at the mirror, needed to look up, but was afraid to face myself. I closed my eyes and my head swam again. When I opened them, I was looking up, looking at myself, and was startled by my bestial appearance. My hair was a wild mat; stubble covered my face like fur. A trail of dried blood painted a track across my forehead and my eyes were red and dead like dull scratched rubies. The guy from the picture, gone through the wringer. My head reeled and I closed my eyes.

With trepidation, I looked down at Win's passport again but he was still not in it. His blonde curls and big handsome face nowhere to be found. Gone. Instead, my picture, with that same passport half smile, stared back at me.

My mind raced. What conspiracy was this that had stuck my picture on Win's passport? What were they trying to accomplish? Where the hell was Win?

I leaned on the counter and looked in the mirror again, and then down at the tiny blood red orchid. Little pinpricks of light started dancing in my eyes, then, there was a blinding flash. My mind reeled and I remembered. I remembered it all.

Jenna in the black cocktail dress, her "O" necklace hanging like a target between her breasts, her legs wrapping around me as I pin her to the wall of her hotel and we sweat. My amuse-bouche.

Me leaving a weak little part of myself back at the coffeeshop, waiting.

Back-alley meetings with unsavory characters and I'm arranging my best one yet. It'll be a good show. All I need is the perfect girl and I'm working on her. I'll find her.

Destiny, her ample body enveloping me, and when I'm done I'm a beast to her, unleashing a torrent of hate and she has no choice but to take it and cry. A weak little part of me waits in the hall, listening, disapproving.

Monica from Atlanta, eyes glazed and drugged and walking out with me into a dark starlight Amsterdam night. She is not the perfect girl, but she is tonight's girl. My appetizer.

Me straddling her by the canal, spent. My hands warm and tingling and I'm savoring the peace as she lies still now and forever.

I lay on the ground at the edge of the canal, looking at the inky blackness below, staring at her face, pale and beautiful and slowly sinking. As the darkness swallows her, my own face comes into view, reflected in the murky water. For a moment, my face and her face become one. Her eyes are my eyes, and I can almost see myself, disheveled, spent, fixated on her. She is sinking into the water and leaving me there alone, staring at my reflection and at Win behind me. I turn to look but Win is not there. It is just me. Alone. Wolves howl and bay in the distance, approving.

Cassie. Cassie. The main course. Cassie. Perfect Cassie. Cassie drinking a tiny beer, unaware of the small white pill dissolving at the bottom.

I puked. All into the sink. I leaned on the counter, bile dribbling down my chin. I shut my eyes and tears seeped out and dripped onto the vanity. It could not have been real. I prayed again for time to turn back, for Cassie to be alive and well and looking at the Van Goghs in Paris at that moment. And the funny thing was, right then, I actually believed that was exactly where she was. That was the only place she could be. I told myself this, looking in the mirror, over and over, until I believed it.

I wiped the tears from my eyes and the spittle from my chin with a towel and shambled to the bedroom. My suitcase sat neatly packed on the bed and the folded printout showing my itinerary sat on top. I picked it up and read it. My flight was in two hours. I stood paralyzed for what surely must have been a minute or longer. There was no way any human in their right mind would let me aboard any aircraft and even if they did there was no way that American Nazi border patrol would let me past the gates without severe rubber-hose questioning at best.

I sloughed off my clothes quickly and ran the shower as hot as it would go and stood under it, letting it redden my skin and disinfect me. I shaved in the shower, leaving what looked like matted wet fur on the shower floor. Wolf fur.

I got out, dried with a stiff used towel and rummaged carefully in the packed suitcase for fresh clothes. I put my old clothes from last night's still-fresh hell in the garbage bin, took the plastic bag out and tied it off, meaning to throw it away into the nearest incinerator or canal. I threw my suitcase closed and did a quick scan of the room, leaving the orchid but taking Win's note and the passport, and bounded down the stairs towards reception with sick dread.

I stood impatiently behind a very feeble elderly couple checking in and finally they were done and I went up to the desk and set my room key down.

"Ah, Mr. Jones, was everything satisfactory?" the clerk asked.

"I'm not Mr. Jones," I said, "that's my friend. Have you seen him?" I was still expecting that Win would return, that the conspiracy would unravel.

The clerk looked at me quizzically. "Mr. Darwin Jones?" he asked.

"Yes, have you seen him?" I asked again, "Tall guy, loud, curly blonde hair?"

The clerk remained silent, confused.

"Oh, never mind," I said impatiently. I needed to catch that flight. "Just give me the damage," I told him.

"Ah," he stuttered, "sure, okay, ah, here is the bill, for your review, please."

I scanned it and aside from Win's enormous room service tab everything looked to be in order. I scrawled my signature.

"Are you feeling okay, Mr. Jones?" the hotel clerk asked and I glared at him. I had to get out. Fast. I grabbed my bag and left, sending the revolving door spinning like a roulette wheel behind me.

I walked quickly with my suitcase clicking behind me on the uneven cobblestones and occasionally twisting crazily when it hit the wrong spot. I hustled and in ten breathless minutes I was at Centraal Station with its beehive of people of every kind coming and going. I dumped the bag with my old clothes in a trashcan and ran up to the platform for the train to Schiphol. I hopped the train without a ticket and prayed the conductor wouldn't come but he did. As he was coming towards me, I casually left and walked the other way like I was going to the bathroom, went to the upper level and circled back around him and sat waiting for him to finish with the car, at which point I rejoined my luggage.

I ran out of the train and up escalator ramps and got my boarding pass from a machine, and went towards security, at which point it occurred to me in a freezing panic that didn't remember packing my suitcase. Had I? I lied to the severe security lady and said I had packed it. No it did not contain any illegal substances. She waved me on.

After I passed security without incident, I went to the bathroom and rummaged around in the suitcase to make sure Win had packed no surprises or care packages. All that was in there, though, were dirty socks and clothes. Then I saw a cupcake in a wrapped paper bag with Win's lunatic writing on it, saying, "Take. Eat." I was suddenly aware that I was ravenously hungry and I ate it greedily in the bathroom stall like a degenerate, knowing that I probably should not eat it but I did anyway in that frenetic morning.

Before long I was at my gate and going through a second round of security, calmer this time, and soon I was on the plane settling in for the long flight. Already everything was hazy and dreamlike and distant. The memories were all receding into the past so fast that I had to keep checking my camera to remind myself of all that had happened. I looked and looked but I couldn't find a single picture of Win. I missed him in a crazy way. A picture of Cassie now came up, beautiful and sunny on the grass at Vondelpark, and my heart leapt to my throat and raced. I prayed to God again and hoped that last night's nightmare had only been a hallucination and that Cassie was still alive and beautiful and that the Devil did not exist and there were no wolves after me and all was well and good in my small happy world.

I began to feel strange and disconnected and very grounded and good with Win's no-doubt laced delectable cupcake. The flight attendant's safety monotone drifted away into meaningless dribble and I stared out the window at the strange and heavy fog that had settled in. Summer was leaving with me and now began the cold long descent into bitter windy winter. Already I longed to return and thought about leaping out of the plane on a yellow inflatable slide. But I didn't leap out. I felt deliciously heavy, like the huge plane I was in, and I settled into the seat.

The pilot taxied and we waited our turn in the long line of planes. One by one I could see them in the fog turning onto the runway. They silently got smaller and lifted into the air without effort as if carried by the very clouds and then they slowly disappeared into the heavy fog. Soon it was our turn and we rolled onto the empty tarmac with long runway lights strobing off into an infinity of fog. We turned and the engines breathed in great gulps of air. I was already flying and the silent power pushed me back in the seat making me even heavier. The strobing lights got closer and closer and closer until they were one light-saber like blur of light and we rose without a sound into the fog and Holland disappeared slowly below me into a misty memory. I shed one more tear and then smiled and closed my eyes and drifted off to sleep and dreamt of baby wolves.

EPILOGUE
ROAD TO AMSTERDAM

Real life – so-called real life – sucks. My reentry into it was rough and it was tough to be responsible and return phone calls and deal with people and not walk around stoned and drunk all day. For a couple of days I puttered around in a funk in my house, not bothering to dress or shower. On the third day after I got back, I finally resolved to dress and go do the errands I needed to do. I stopped by work, checked messages, and sent out emails, but quickly left for the bank, eager to get it done.

I entered the lobby and put my name on the little sheet and soon I was ushered off to the vault on the side of the bank to the safe deposit boxes. I took the key from my pocket and in a moment the box sat on the round table like a tiny metal coffin. I waited for the attendant to leave, then quickly opened it. I was aching to leave the claustrophobic place. I threw in my passport and a tiny 2" x 2" picture of a girl fell out. Or was it two pictures stuck together? It was hard to tell and I did not want to linger and find out. I slammed the lid of the metal box shut and put it back in its slot. Just another number now.

I hurried home after the bank, eager to sit in solitude in my bathrobe all day. Upon my return, I discovered an email from Cassie that read:

"Paris is awesome. The Monets are incredible. Wish you were here. Cass xoxo"

I breathed a tremendous sigh of relief when I read this. If I hadn't received it, I would have probably faked a message and sent it to myself just to feel better.

I wrote her a few emails, sometimes long emails, but I never received anything from her but short, cryptic answers. I thought it was probably best if I didn't call her. We were literally as far as the East from the West anyway. I tried separating my wonderful sun-dappled memories of her on that perfect day from the surreal blood horrors of that last night, which hopefully, I still prayed, were only a hallucination. I could not separate the two, so I didn't think about her much and she slowly receded into forgotten memories. Time is linear and relentless and the cruelest thing I know, but sometimes She throws you a bone and swallows something that no one else could have.

I managed to get a draft of my Christian travel book to my editor in the nick of time, thanks to a Michelin guide that I cribbed mercilessly, lots of Yahoo! searches and my own hazy recollections of the trip. My first draft was a disaster and read simply, "Amsterdam for Christians: don't come." But that was not right. There was a lot of Christian history and art and music there all touched by a spark of the divine, not to mention the fact that the city, and the tourists more directly, really needed help if that was your bent as a Christian. In any case, Frederick and his partners liked it very much and, after some additions and revisions, "Road to Amsterdam" was done.

A week after I turned in the final draft, I threw a wine tasting party at home to celebrate. Actually, it was a thinly veiled excuse to get hammered among friends where I wouldn't have to drive, and also I secretly liked the attention. I ran into Frederick.

"You should write another one," Frederick said. "Ever been to Venice?"

"Nope. Sounds great though," I said, taking a great big gulp of my Pinot Gris. Somewhere far away, and audible only if you could be quiet enough, Win gave a tremendous howl that echoed on and on.

Acknowledgements

A sincere "thank you" goes out to all those who made this book possible. You, my friends, share in the blame. In all seriousness, without your edits and suggestions, and your courageous reading of my first draft, this book would not be.

Another sincere "thank you" goes to the city of Amsterdam itself, and, specifically, the many bars that fueled my writing. It really is a wonderful place, full of the nicest and most forgiving people on the planet.

L.G. RIVERA

Dammed

.G. Rivera was born in Spain and loves to travel. From the top f the Eiffel Tower to the impoverished slums of Haiti, he finds eauty and darkness anywhere he goes. He lives in Florida and is ie author of three novels and multiple short stories. His next ovel, AGOBIO, is scheduled for release in 2013. You can find iore information at www.lgrivera.com.